damsel in (social) distance

damsel in (social) distance

C.P. Morgan

Special Thanks to

*Eleni McKnight, Karin Mitchell, Morgan Hazelwood,
Carol Vaughn, Kris McClain, La Kata Kling, Quasar
Morris, Dr. Elizabeth Julius, and Mary Armen.*

day 1

Daisy Colton's entire life fit inside six boxes and two suitcases. The culmination of twenty-eight years lay wrapped in used plastic grocery bags buffeted by books and old movies. The last remnants of a life she tried not to believe was completely wasted. With tear-stained cheeks, she grabbed the last box from her white sedan, pausing just long enough to take a deep breath. The tears brimmed her eyes again, but these were different. They were tears of relief. She was safe. She was home. Time would heal her wounds, and she would get through this—pandemic or no.

She balanced the last box on her hip as she closed the trunk and headed up the garden-lined drive to her childhood home. The screen door slammed behind her and the butter-yellow walls of the living room greeted her. It was nearly impossible to feel anything but cozy and comfortable in the Colton's one-story, suburban home. Exactly how her mother would have wanted it.

Her old bedroom was like a time capsule, preserved under a thin layer of dust, only occasionally disturbed by her mother's annual spring cleaning. Baby pink walls peeked from beneath old Avril Lavigne posters, now faded and sun-bleached, and the collage of magazine clippings of Orlando Bloom that still clung to the corkboard by her bed.

A knock reverberated on the door, and Daisy's mother poked her head in.

"I'm off to work," Mrs. Colton said, her voice cheery, her equally cheery face framed by a short blonde bob.

Daisy slouched. "I can't believe you still have to work with everything going on."

"People still need their medications filled, Sunshine."

"I know," Daisy sighed, setting the box she still carried on her lacey duvet. "I'm worried about you."

"Don't be." Mrs. Colton took Daisy's hands with a reassuring squeeze. "When you're done unpacking, why don't you go take a walk? You're free. Enjoy it."

"Go outside? In a pandemic? Do you have enough disinfectant wipes for the entire uptown district of Erie River, then?"

Mrs. Colton patted her daughter's cheek. "You know I do. I love you, Sunshine."

"Love you too."

Daisy sank into her mother's embrace. It was the kind that came without conditions or repercussions. She clung to the woman's shoulders almost like a child, worried it was perhaps too long. Mrs. Colton did not break free of Daisy's hold. She smiled at her daughter when she pulled away, tucking a strand of platinum-blonde hair behind her daughter's ear.

As the bedroom door closed again, the momentary strength Daisy had taken from her mother vanished. Leaving had been the easy part. Facing what she'd left behind was something she hadn't prepared for. Among the dusty remains of her past were several pieces of dated jewelry strewn across her dresser and pictures she barely remembered.

Her ex held her on his back at a college party. Her ex stood between her and her friends as they posed for one last photo before she left for Arizona. Her ex smiled at the camera, lifting a beer in a kind of salute. Daisy ripped the photograph in half, her hands shaking as she made her way to the trash can and paused.

She couldn't do it. Eric had been the only man who ever loved her. The only one who ever would. She opened her dresser and shoved the picture between the bundles of old toe-socks and underwear. She had to break free of his hold on her. That's why she left, why she came back home. To find a way, her way, away from him. She knew it wouldn't be easy, but for her own sanity, she had to try.

Daisy shoved the drawer closed. Nope. She was *not* going there. *The past was in the past,* she scolded herself. Pulling off the sweaty shirt she'd worn for two days, Daisy donned a pair of snowflake pajama bottoms and her alma mater sweater. It was still her favorite, despite being tattered and covered in paint splatter. The unpacking could wait.

In the kitchen, the sunflower backsplash lay hidden behind an odd assortment of items Mrs. Colton felt fit to keep on hand. The piles of yellowing mail and decades' worth of countertop gadgets clashed with the stainless-steel appliances, giving the place a less cozy and more lived-in feel. Daisy pulled a pint of ice cream from the freezer, retreating to the less cluttered living room and the sanctuary of the familiar heather-gray sofa.

"… wash hands often, and avoid touching your eyes, nose, and mouth."

Daisy changed the channel and shoved another too-large bite of ice cream into her mouth.

"Under the stay-at-home order, all non-essential businesses should now be closed."

Change. Swallow.

"… the elderly and anyone with immune deficiencies are more likely to have complications."

Change. Bite.

"… and being careful with what you bring into your homes. We do not know how long this lockdown will last, but if we all do our part, the sooner we can stop the spread, the sooner we can get back to the way things were. It looks like the governor is preparing to speak—"

The ice cream pint was more than half gone. So, this was how the Quarantine Fifteen occurred. Daisy licked the spoon one last time and secured the lid. With messages from the CDC and other commercials ringing in her mind, she returned the ice cream to the freezer. Taking inventory of the household's supply of disinfectant wipes and soap seemed important. And it kept her from unearthing more memories in her bedroom.

Daisy crouched on the floor, looking into the depths of the cabinet beneath the kitchen sink. Why did it always seem like the darkest place in existence? It was impossible to see all the way to the back without banging into a pipe or missing a bottle of something altogether. She found a single container of wipes and tucked it beneath her arm. Pulling out her phone, she used a wipe to clean its surface, and then her hands, before shining the flashlight toward the back of the cabinet. There, she extracted a large, refill container of hand soap, and a dried-out package of more disinfectant wipes.

The front door opened and closed, and Daisy pulled her head out of the cabinet.

"Mom?" she called hesitantly. "Did you forget—"

Daisy screamed as a giant, fluffy dog plowed into her. She threw up her arms, waiting for the feel of teeth to sink into her flesh.

Many believe that fate comes in like a shining beacon. That, in this moment, destiny feels like a person is exactly where they're supposed to be, and doing exactly what they're supposed to be doing. Fate, destiny, prophecy, for it has many names, is like the spark that lights a brilliant firework deep within, bursting with an all-powerful knowing and assurance.

"Apollo! Off!"

The sniffing nose and sloppy kisses ceased, and Daisy looked up at Fate not with an all-powerful knowing, but with fuming anger and shock as a man held the collar of the wiggling dog before her.

"Who the—who are you? What are you doing in my house?" Daisy demanded, trying to both stand and shrink into the counter.

"I'm so sorry. I didn't realize anyone was home."

Daisy recoiled from the proffered hand before taking in the man it was attached to. Gentle hazel eyes looked down at her as a muscular build held the wagging dog at bay. Bulging biceps threatened to rip the sleeves of the black and white shirt that clung tight to his arms, and a strand of dark brown hair fell across his forehead like a 90s boy band heartthrob.

"I'm Luke. Luke Richards," the man continued, dropping his hand and switching out which arm restrained the dog. "This is Apollo. He won't hurt you, promise. He'll just lick your face off until you scratch his ears."

"Are you crazy? What are you doing in my house?" Daisy asked again, her voice more authoritative this time.

"I didn't know anyone was home. I'm a dog walker in the uptown area. Your mom lets me use her yard for playdates. I—I'm assuming she's your mom. You look just like her."

Daisy raised an eyebrow. "Excuse me?"

"In a good way! I mean, not that I'm into your mom." Luke ran a hand over his face.

"Yes, she's my mother. How did you not know I was here? I parked my car in the middle of the driveway. And what if I hadn't been dressed!"

"Yes, that would have been..." Luke's gaze slid down Daisy's frame with her winter pajama bottoms and hole-covered sweater. "… terrible." He tried to hide his smile, hazel eyes roving back up the woman before him and locking her chocolate rich eyes with his. "I'm sorry I didn't see your car. I don't usually come up the driveway. I came through the side yard." He pointed out the bay window of the parlor, barely visible through the kitchen doorway. "Apollo and I live across the street."

"I don't care where you live. Just check the driveway next time."

"So, you're saying there's a next time?" Luke asked, his voice rising with anticipation.

"Whatever," Daisy huffed, crossing her arms. "I don't know what kind of arrangement my mother has with you, but I expect you to ring the doorbell, not barge in here like you own the place."

"Deal."

Daisy grabbed the container of disinfectant wipes and stormed out of the kitchen with indignation. She stopped in the hall, backtracking until she stood framed in the doorway. "Wait a minute. This is *my* house. Why am I leaving?"

"I don't know. Why are you leaving?" Luke said, now fully smiling in amusement.

"I'm not, that's my point. You leave."

"As you wish." With his free hand placed across his chest, Luke bowed, whispering a command in Apollo's ear. The dog lowered his front, and placed his head on his paws, tail still wagging in the air.

It was stupidly adorable, and Daisy had to force herself to hold her firm expression. As Luke stood again, she recognized the design on his shirt as the tree of Gondor. Did he know he was wearing a *Lord of the Rings* shirt?

Luke pulled back his shoulders, still holding firm to Apollo's collar. "My lady, I would wish to fulfill the task you've set for me, but you see, a beautiful maiden has barred my path. Might you permit a man and his noble companion to pass?"

Daisy's lips parted slightly. Clearing her throat, she stepped to the side and unbarred the kitchen doorway. Luke inclined his head again and led Apollo toward the front door. As he passed, Daisy inhaled, taking in the scent of bergamot and oakmoss, and felt a wave flush through her body.

"And keep your dog on a leash!" she called, her voice breaking.

It was several seconds after the front door closed did Daisy's legs finally allow her to move. She scrambled to the sink, scrubbing her hands, neck, and face of dried dog slobber. She continued to scrub, forcing her heartbeat to calm. She'd scrub her entire body if she had to until the memory of those hazel eyes and the scent of Luke's cologne had been replaced with the scent of lemon dish soap.

Something had happened to her, and she couldn't explain it. If this was what it felt like to recover from almost a decade of psychological abuse, Daisy was vastly unprepared.

No, she told herself, *she only felt this way because he was the first man she'd met since leaving Eric.*

But it wasn't true. She'd encountered plenty of young men at gas stations and rest areas along her route from Arizona to Ohio. He wasn't the first. So why did the world seem to fall away beneath her feet when she looked at him?

Daisy abandoned her attempts at the sink. She pulled the half-eaten pint of ice cream from the freezer again and returned to the couch. Her heart still beat, and the scent of Luke's cologne lingered in her mind, no matter how hard she scrubbed with the kitchen soap.

"Citizens are advised to stay home and practice social distancing as much as possible." The governor was still speaking.

With each bite of ice cream, Daisy wasn't sure if her fear was growing or subsiding. She couldn't imagine being quarantined with Eric. She was sure he would have used the situation to his advantage, to further control her in some way. How much more control he could have gained, she shuddered to think. And if the one man in the whole world who would ever or could ever love Daisy Colton could do all that to her, what could another man do?

As the governor referred a reporter's question to one of his specialists, Daisy heard Apollo's distinct bark from across the street. Eric would have never called her a beautiful maiden.

The sky was black when Mrs. Colton returned home. A single streetlamp illuminated a tiny patch of sidewalk that faded into the night in either direction, empty and lonely. She fumbled with the door handle against a mask and oversized handbag in one hand, the other clutching a large, brown paper bag of Chinese takeout.

"Hey, Sunshine," she greeted Daisy, her eyes roving over the empty ice cream container and several old Halloween candy wrappers scattered across the coffee table. "How was your day?"

"Mom! Are you crazy!" Daisy sprung from the couch, brandishing the disinfectant wipes like a banner. She wiped down the door handle, her mother's keys, and each container in the paper bag.

"Daisy, relax. You know the Yang's. They're being very safe. Social distancing and everything. You should have seen the little boxes they taped on the floor—"

"That's not the point. People can be silent carriers,

Mom. *Speaking* of which." Daisy discarded the disinfectant wipes and scrubbed her hands at the kitchen sink as Mrs. Colton made room on the crowded breakfast nook. "Letting a stranger and his dog walk through our house? What are you thinking?

"Oh, you met Luke! Good!"

"Good? It is not good. They scared me to death! How could you forget to tell me some guy and his giant dog were coming over?"

Mrs. Colton unwrapped a pair of wooden chopsticks, unloading the little white cartons amongst the overflowing assortment of mail and treasures long forgotten on the table. "I'm sorry I forgot, Sunshine. You didn't exactly give me much notice you were coming. I love having you back, but I did forget today was his day to come over."

"What if I wasn't dressed?"

"Weren't you?"

"Of course I was, but—"

"Then what's there to worry about?" Mrs. Colton popped a wonton in her mouth, barely chewing before swallowing.

"He could have killed me!

"Luke is a very sweet man."

"Mom, I thought he was a burglar!"

"With a key?"

Daisy stared, blinking at her mother. "How was I supposed to know he had a key?"

"How was I supposed to know my daughter might

have been spending her day hanging out in her birthday suit?"

"*Mom!*" Years of repressed anger, the inability to defend herself, and who knew what else made it difficult to keep calm. The anxiety of the looming pandemic she'd spent the entire day listening to and watching didn't help matters.

"Sunshine, I promise, Luke is not a stranger. He'd good as harm my tulips than hurt you or anyone. And Apollo is just a big, fluffy goofball. Luke walks several dogs in the neighborhood. He can let the dogs loose to play for a half-hour—"

"That fluffy goofball bowled me over like a feather when he came charging in here," Daisy cut her mother's rambling short.

Mrs. Colton chuckled, slurping at another wonton in her soup.

"It's not funny! Do you even *know* what the statistic are saying about this pandemic right now? What our chances of contracting it and *dying* are?"

Mrs. Colton sighed, pushing the empty plastic container of soup away from her. "Yes, I am very much aware of what's going on. I work at a pharmacy." She gestured at her blue lab coat. "But this pandemic is why human connection will be more important now than ever. Besides, Luke isn't a stranger. Not to me. And he's a paramedic. He knows about pandemic safety."

"A paramedic? Mom, don't you know it's health professionals who are most at risk?" Hours of interviews with doctors, nurses, and government officials rang through Daisy's mind. "If he catches it and brings it in here… I didn't leave my life in Arizona just to die of a stupid virus!"

"You're not going to die. Do you hear me? Luke is not going to bring the virus into the house."

Daisy shoved an egg roll in her mouth, though food was the last thing her body wanted after consuming hours of televised fear and a steady supply of sugar.

"You know," Mrs. Colton continued once Daisy's mouth was thoroughly preoccupied with her egg roll, "he might be just the guy to get you over Eric."

"Wha—no, no." Daisy quickly chewed her egg roll, swallowing it more whole than was probably safe. "I have no interest in a new relationship, and I probably never will."

But, man, did he smell good.

"Daisy, you listen to me right now. Do *not* let Eric break you. Do not let whatever that boy did, whatever happened, define you."

Daisy stared back at her mother, feeling her eyes sting with the threat of tears.

"Promise me."

"I promise," Daisy whispered.

"I love you so much, Daisy, and I never want anyone to keep you from me ever again."

Daisy shifted in her seat, staring at the unopened takeout container in front of her. "It was my fault I didn't call. Or visit. I… I was embarrassed."

"It was not your fault, Daisy. And you have nothing to be embarrassed about."

"I wanted to make you and Papa proud."

"Your Papa was so proud of you, Sunshine. And so am I. So proud."

Daisy shook her head. "But I did nothing with my life. My degree was a waste."

Pushing a pile of mail away, Mrs. Colton grabbed Daisy's hand. "It was not a waste. And neither are you. You'll see it one day."

Daisy studied the takeout container until she felt she could see through its waxy, cardboard layer to the food that lay inside. Her mother was wrong, blinded by parental instinct. Four years of art school and nothing to show for it. A comprehensive examination of art throughout history and how science and engineering advances influenced the progression of art culture wasn't exactly typical dinner conversation. And though she also minored in French and Latin, neither of those were of much use in Arizona or Ohio.

Four years of Daisy's life had been utterly wasted, and she was lucky to have found work at all. It had been Eric who found her a job, not Daisy, and it was Eric who took care of their day-to-day life. Because understanding anatomy, ceramics, and the composition of oil paints did not prepare you for reading a utility bill.

"Hey, let's go watch a movie," Mrs. Colton broke the silence. "Whatever you want to watch."

Daisy grinned as the suggestion pulled her from the well of darkness she had begun descending. "Return of the King?" The sight of the tree of Gondor stretched across a firm chest seemed to give her inspiration.

"That's the one with the hotty from your wall, right?"

"Mom, I was, like, fifteen when I put those up," Daisy laughed.

They retreated to the living room, arranging the little white takeout containers on the coffee table amongst the empty ice cream pint and candy wrappers.

"Yeah, and they're still up, aren't they?" Mrs. Colton teased.

Daisy tried desperately to think of a comeback, but it wasn't Orlando Bloom's face that swam before her mind's eye. Her silence seemed to invite her mother to tickle her ribs, and Daisy squealed and laughed like she was twelve again. She fell off the heather-gray sofa, nearly upending Mrs. Colton's chicken lo Mein.

"Okay! Okay! Truce! White flag! I surrender!" she laughed.

Mrs. Colton released her daughter's ribs, helping her back onto the sofa and straightening the food containers. She popped a pot sticker in her mouth from a container that still teetered precariously on the edge of the table.

"I'm so happy you're home," Mrs. Colton whispered, kissing her daughter's forehead as Daisy snuggled into her. "Whatever the reason."

day 2

Sleep came easily to Daisy that night. More easily than it had for many years. With her head cradled in her mother's lap, Daisy fell asleep to the sound of battles and Ian McKellen's voice as a backing track to her dreams. She dreamed of a muscular soldier with hazel eyes and a wisp of hair that fell across his face. She dreamed of falling from a tall tower, falling through a layer of ice, falling from the precipice of the White City of Gondor.

She stretched and yawned as the sun fell across her face, pulling her from a passionate dream-rendezvous with a hazel-eyed knight astride a black dragon that looked oddly similar to Apollo. Her eyes fluttered open, and she found herself wrapped in her father's favorite afghan, and her mother already gone to work. She stared out the window at the birds that flitted around the birdfeeder in the garden outside the parlor window.

So, this was freedom. A chill seemed to run the

length of her body, through her skin, her muscles, into her very soul as realization sank in. She had no obligations to do anything today, and with it, the absence of what had become such a part of her life. There was no nagging fear of what mistakes she'd make today. No questioning every movement, every facial expression, every lilt in syllable spoken. The feeling was light and hollow. The feeling was empty.

Daisy sat up, scanning the living room around her. She felt like a bystander, looking in from somewhere else, perhaps from her dream world, and not a part of the essence of this plane at all. She knew fear. She knew apprehension. She knew how to ebb and flow with the monsters at the back of her mind and the pit of her stomach. Now that she was free, now that it was gone, it was like a piece of Daisy was too.

Still groggy, Daisy threw off her father's afghan and padded down the hall to her bedroom. She grabbed one of the unopened boxes from her room, setting it before the large bay window in the parlor. From its depths, she unpacked a foldable easel and a blank canvas. Anxiety rose in her stomach. It was the last canvas she purchased before finishing art school. Eric had scolded her for wanting to buy more. She could never bring herself to use it, to waste it on a mistake.

Taking a breath, Daisy set the canvas on the easel. Today she would make a mistake. And she would come out the other side whole. She paused only a moment before setting the brush loaded with paint to the canvas. It was as natural as breathing. The increase and decrease in pressure of the bristles against the textured canvas surface. Mixing colors to make new, exotic splashes amongst the spring greens and emeralds. Before her eyes, the garden, with its little golden finches and red-breasted robins, materialized. Before her eyes, her mistake took shape. The yellow of the golden finch wasn't quite right. One petal on the tulip was slightly too large. The shading of the forget-me-not's stem was off, extending too far, and too dark in color. It was a beautiful and glorious mistake of a canvas filled with dozens of tiny mistakes.

A knock on the front door brought Daisy out of her world of watercolors and into the vivid, sharpened lines of reality. She wiped the paint from her hands onto her sweater and tied a bandana around her nose and mouth. Peering through the peephole, Luke's muscular physique stood on her front step. Apollo sat at his side, fully leashed.

Daisy opened the door a crack.

"Hi," Luke said tentatively, wiping the strand of hair that fell across his forehead out of his eyes.

"Can I help you?" Daisy asked, watching Apollo's tail wag faster.

"You asked me to knock the next time we stopped by."

"I... I suppose I did."

"Are you dressed today?"

Daisy's brow furrowed. "Of course I am! What kind

of question is that?"

"It was one of your concerns. Can we come in?"

Daisy's heart beat faster. What was wrong with her? His hazel eyes met hers, and she felt a vigor run through her—nope. No. No, and definitely not.

"Oh, here." Luke pulled a mask from his pocket, slipping the straps over his ears and adjusting it around his nose. "They don't make dog ventilators within my budget, I'm afraid."

Daisy's brow relaxed. She stifled a laugh, glad for the bandana as she held the door open for her guests. Apollo stayed close to Luke's side, but his tail seemed to have a mind of its own. Daisy closed the door, putting some distance between her and Luke, which only made Apollo advance toward her even more.

"Does—does he bite?" Daisy asked, holding her hands close to her chest.

"Not unless I tell him to. Don't worry. You've done nothing to warrant a bite from my fierce messenger of the dog gods."

Paint-stained fingers gently touched the dog's head. He was so soft. Daisy felt her shoulders relax as Apollo turned his head to lick her wrist. He wiggled and whimpered as if fighting some inner force that kept him from completely assaulting her with his doggy affections.

"You paint?" Luke asked.

"Huh?" Daisy turned to the parlor, hoping her canvas of mistakes wasn't in view.

Luke shook his head and reached for Daisy's hand. Their fingers barely touched before Daisy pulled away, her heart fluttering as the scent of bergamot and oakmoss met her again.

"Your hands," Luke said, dropping his own to his sides again. "And your shirt. There are a few more spots than yesterday."

"Oh... it's, um."

A strand of hair fell across Luke's forehead again, and he shook his head a bit, tossing it back into place.

Six feet, Daisy. Six feet.

Her body had inched its way toward Luke, her awareness of self, space, and time lost as their eyes found each other. She felt her face blush and took a step back.

"It's just a hobby," she said.

Luke cleared his throat, his eyes finding a spot on Apollo's leash to study instead. "Your mom told me you went to art school."

"So, you talk to my mother about me often?" Crossing her arms, Daisy felt the flush in her face diminish and her senses of constraint and control return.

"She talks to me about you."

"Oh," Daisy mumbled, as the years of silence between her and her family finally reared their head.

"I don't mind. Your mother's always been kind to me. She even buys Apollo a toy for Christmas, huh, boy?"

The dog barked at his owner's acknowledgement.

"Yeah, that's something she'd do," Daisy mumbled.

Silence fell between them as the weight of a thousand mistakes fell onto Daisy's shoulders, mistakes that weren't as simple as the wrong color yellow on a tiny painter's canvas.

"Well, backyard's this way. Good day, Miss Daisy."

Luke bowed to her as he had done the day before, guiding Apollo through the kitchen and toward the back door. Daisy watched them go, her guilt turning to frustration when she found her eyes lingering on Luke's backside. She ripped the bandana from her face and stormed into the kitchen. Could she have been more obvious? More stupid? As the back door closed, she found a determination to release her anger in what she hoped was a more productive way than staring at the back of her neighbor's jeans.

The kitchen was a rather tiny space, but Mrs. Colton had managed to fit dozens of appliances, stacks of papers and cookbooks, and even Daisy's childhood ocarina onto the depths of the counter. Daisy grabbed the box that had contained her art supplies and began sorting the contents of the kitchen as the sounds of Luke and Apollo's play filled the air.

He was handsome, she'd admit that much. But the last time she committed to the first man who ever gave her attention, it hadn't ended the way she'd planned. Daisy was barely seventeen when she began dating the cute boy who worked at the ice cream shop on Dame Street. Everyone said they looked good together. Everyone said Eric was the most popular boy at their small-town high school. Everyone said how lucky Daisy was that he'd even noticed her. Everyone said… as Daisy stood by and said nothing.

She said nothing when Eric said her prom dress was too old-fashioned, that she needed to show more skin, said otherwise it would be her fault if they didn't win homecoming King and Queen. She said nothing when Eric told her where they'd live after college, what jobs she could and couldn't have. And she said nothing when she realized the dependent situation she'd gotten herself into, ashamed and afraid to call her parents and ask for help. She couldn't even bring herself to speak up when Eric demanded they leave immediately after her father's funeral instead of staying for a few days to help her mother.

Yes, mistakes on a canvas were one thing, and accepting one's mistakes were fine and well. But when those mistakes rippled out like a stone thrown into Lake Erie, silence could no longer be an option, and the consequences were yet to be seen.

Daisy started at one end of the kitchen counter, sorting out piles of junk mail and filtering through several dust-covered appliances. She'd never seen her mother use the food processor in her life, and yet it sat there on display since before Daisy was born. She gathered all its bits and pieces and tossed it into the box. A broken coffee maker, a set of brittle plastic measuring spoons, and a sack of forgotten potatoes later, one corner of the counter was spotless for the first time in ages.

Satisfied for the time being, Daisy washed her hands—twice for good measure—and secured her paints and brushes. The painting that sat upon the easel was more beautiful than she remembered, its mistakes creating an intentional kind of charm. She smiled, proud of the way the yellow finch's colors stood out against the pale, blue sky. But the feeling was fleeting. She turned away as another voice forced its way in, filling her mind with a dark cloud.

"Daisy, you know painting will never be more than a hobby. You're just not good enough. No one would buy it. You'd have to study in Paris or Venice for years, and you know we don't have that kind of money. I work really hard for us to live here. All you think about is yourself."

"Did you paint that?" Luke asked from behind her.

Daisy jumped, and the painting wobbled on the easel. "Uh, yeah, but it's… it was just something I did this morning. It's not very—"

"It's amazing! You're really talented."

"Oh."

Luke grabbed Apollo's head in his hands, flapping the dog's cheeks and changing his voice like a cartoon character. "Thank you for letting me play in your yard, Miss Daisy."

Daisy smiled, stepping in front of the easel. "You're welcome."

"Farewell, Miss Daisy," Luke said, tipping an imaginary hat, and closing the front door behind him.

Daisy let out a long breath. Why did she freeze around him like some flighty rabbit? Yes, he was cute. Yes, he was charming. Yes, he liked animals.

"Stop it," Daisy commanded aloud. She would not allow herself to fall into that trap again. Besides, she wasn't even sure if Luke knew the shirt he wore yesterday was the tree of Gondor. However, there was nothing stopping her from thinking about what might be hiding beneath those blue jeans. This time, she didn't hide her smile.

The rampage of house cleaning continued through to six o'clock. When more than half of the kitchen counter was visible once again, Daisy fell onto the heather-gray sofa and flipped on the news. The thought of the current pandemic terrified her, but she wanted to stay informed. She *needed* to stay informed. New information was coming out every day. She'd lived through the scares of H1N1, Avian Flu, Swine Flu. But this was something different entirely.

Once upon a time, her greatest fear had been losing her mother to a robbery at the pharmacy. Drug addicts were known to become desperate and seek out the closest corner outlet for a fix. But that story had changed. Now, it was her mother catching this mysterious illness, dying alone in a makeshift hospital ward with a ventilator down her throat. Daisy would surely be next. Could she take care of herself if the worst happened? She was younger and in good health. Perhaps she could avoid the hospital all together. Or would she have to beg Eric to take her back, pretend her leaving was just another gigantic mistake, so she had someone to take care of her?

Daisy found herself standing before the refrigerator, opening the door for what she knew was the third time, but it only just registered. Lacking any will to cook, she dug out a frozen lasagna and set it in the oven to bake. Despite wanting to watch the news, Daisy instead scribbled a grocery list on a sticky note pad she'd unearthed. If the world was going to go into complete lock down, she wanted to be prepared. Canned goods, dry goods, she underlined soap and rubbing alcohol three times, and added dog treats to the bottom of the list with a little flourish.

Just in case.

The oven dinged, but Mrs. Colton still wasn't home. Pushing away the pit in her stomach, Daisy helped herself to a sizeable corner piece and returned to the comfort of the heather-gray sofa.

The news anchors had moved on to a story concerning filing for unemployment. Daisy knew she'd have to do that soon too. Only her boss had known she had planned to leave and gave Daisy her pay early—in cash. It was enough to get her from Arizona to Ohio, plus a little for emergencies. The thought of *The Modern Plate* being closed was almost enough for Daisy to return the money to Misha. She loved her job, even if it didn't pay as much as Eric would have liked.

She changed the channel, flying past crime shows, several 80s action movies, and plenty of sports shows. Of course, finding something like *The Neverending Story* wasn't going to happen, but if she never had to watch another football game again, Daisy would thank the TV gods every day. She wasn't sure if the lack of good television content or how every paltry thing reminded her of him troubled her more. She settled on Shelley Duvall's *The Princess and the Pea* on a retro television station as the front door opened.

"Hello, Sunshine!" Mrs. Colton called.

"Hey, Mom!"

"Don't worry. I see the wipes. I'm disinfecting everything."

"Thanks," Daisy replied sheepishly. "There's lasagna in the kitchen!"

"Fabulous! I'm starving!" Mrs. Colton's footsteps followed the hall to the kitchen. And stopped. "Uh Daisy, what's this?"

"What's what?" Daisy set her plate on the coffee table and joined her mother in the kitchen. The older woman gestured widely at the space.

"Oh, um… yeah. I did a little decluttering."

"A little?"

"Mom, you have to admit, you don't need all this stuff. You're turning into a hoarder. Look, does this coffee machine even work? If it did, why did you get a new one?"

"No, you're right. I've been meaning to throw that

one out. But there's nothing wrong with the food processor."

"Does it work?" Daisy raised an eyebrow at her mother, crossing her arms.

"I'm sure it does."

"I don't think I've ever seen you use it."

"I don't, but it was a wedding present."

"Mom, Papa's been gone for a long time."

"That's not the point, Daisy." Mrs. Colton raised her own eyebrow, matching her daughter's crossed arms and grounded stance.

"If you won't use it, then why have it?"

Mrs. Colton sighed. The lines on her face from the mask she wore all day seemed to grow redder. She pulled her daughter into a hug, surprising Daisy, who leaned into her mother with her back bent, and her arms pinned to her sides.

"Some memories we want to forget. And some memories we don't want to believe are over."

Daisy shifted and sank into her mother's embrace, tears wetting the woman's blue lab coat.

"Hey, hey. What's the matter, Sunshine?"

Daisy sniffed and pulled back. "I don't know. I... I don't know why I'm crying. I'm sorry."

"Don't be sorry, Sunshine. It's okay."

"No, it's not okay. *I'm* not okay. I'm so lost, Mama. Lost and scared, and crying won't fix it! I'm so stupid."

With a gentle hand, Mrs. Colton wiped her daughter's tears, and held Daisy's face in her hands.

"You are not stupid, do you hear me? You are smart and talented, and I don't want to hear that boy's words come out of your mouth again, understand?"

Daisy's lip trembled. She nodded, pulling away and wiping the tears from her face. "Oh, I made a grocery list for you." She cleared her throat, removing the sticky note from her pocket. "Can you go to the store soon?"

"I'll go when I have a day off," Mrs. Colton said, taking her daughter's cue to change the subject. "Or you could go. I picked you up a couple masks, and some gloves."

"I guess I could," Daisy said, trying to push away the anxiety that threatened to bring up the perfectly good lasagna that sat in her stomach. "Thanks."

Mrs. Colton's eyes narrowed as she studied the list. "Dog treats?"

"Don't start. I thought it would be a nice gesture." Daisy said, brandishing a finger at her mother.

"I knew you'd like him," Mrs. Colton said coyly.

"I'm not looking for a new relationship."

"Then what about a friend?"

Daisy plucked the grocery list from her mother's hand. "I don't need a friend, either."

Mrs. Colton raised a knowing eyebrow. Daisy rolled her eyes, pushing past her mother and folding herself into the comfort of the sofa.

day 3

Chef Andrew Souchen was the chef de cuisine at *The Modern Plate.* His credentials and accolades spanned over five decades, three countries, and seven states. He expedited his kitchen with a firm hand, but jovial demeanor, often threatening to loudly serenade a chef that wasn't getting food to the window quickly enough. He had a round, red face, and a deep, belly laugh that reminded Daisy of her father. And he was one of her favorite people in the entire world.

"No, no. Like this, little chef. Hold this part with your little finger. Just like that," he would say while showing her how to make tortellini.

"Let your arm make the knife do the work, little chef. Your hand is there to guide its movement," he would say as he showed her how to properly use a knife.

Every third Tuesday, *The Modern Plate* closed for deep cleaning, and for Chef Andrew to put together new monthly specials. Daisy always volunteered for

Deep Clean Day. Not because the pay was anything substantial, but because Chef Andrew would let Daisy help in the kitchen after her shift had ended.

She learned to clean mussels and dice an onion. She learned to tell the temperature of steak just by feel and filet a fish. She learned food costs, and when it was appropriate to buy certain product out of season, and when it wasn't. It was a game for Daisy, and she absorbed every piece of information like a cactus in the rainy season. Plating, however, was Daisy's favorite part. It was like a ceramic canvas with food instead of paint.

"All the colors must complement each other, but not all at once," he would say when showing her how to use negative space in plating. "Ah, yes. Very good, little chef. I think you're onto something here. Let's see what the managers think. Maybe we can use it during service next week."

During yet another purge of the kitchen, Daisy unearthed an old avocado-green crock-pot. She wiped off the dust and plugged it in. It still worked. She scrounged through the cupboards and freezer as the crock-pot warmed up, pulling out honey, a pork loin, and several spices that had fallen to the back of a cabinet.

Soon, the aroma of barbeque pulled pork filled the house, thanks to one of Chef Andrew's recipes. It was a welcome distraction from the dismal task of scrolling through Arizona's unemployment website. Daisy wasn't sure Ohio's would have been much better. She finally found the correct filing link and watched her mouse cursor turn to a spinning wheel.

"Who's a good boy? Who's the goodest boy?"

Daisy gazed out the parlor window, watching as Apollo greeted Luke at his front door. The fluffy dog bounded in circles around the man's legs before zooming from one end of the drive to the other. Luke was dressed in his black paramedic uniform, a mask still hanging around his neck. The black, button-up shirt, emblazoned with a variety of patches and symbols, was like a collage of coat of arms. But that wasn't what Daisy found herself enjoying about the short-sleeved and well-fitted uniform.

Luke looked up, smiling at Daisy when he saw her staring, and waved. Daisy sat straighter, slamming her laptop lid closed before waving back in a kind of robotic gesture. Luke herded Apollo through the front door, leaving Daisy staring at the back of her laptop screen in exasperation.

"What is *wrong* with you?" she said before opening the laptop and loading the unemployment website again.

Once more, the cursor turned into a little spinning dial. Maybe she should have just called. She grabbed her cell phone and noticed a social media message from a Lucas Henry Richards. She held her breath and selected the message. A picture of Apollo with a fake rose in his mouth popped up. The caption beneath it read:

Luke: Apollo says he's sorry about scaring you the other day.

Daisy stared back at the picture, a smile curling the corners of her lips.

Daisy: Maybe you need to teach Apollo about social distancing.

A speech bubble bounced up and down as Luke typed a response.

Luke: Apollo is only good at social distancing so long as you keep throwing the ball.

Daisy giggled, but the smile that came to her fell as a sudden realization struck her. Her thumbs flew across the phone's keyboard, and she pressed Send.

Daisy: How did you find me?

At the first rest stop she'd come to, Daisy had locked down her social media account. Unfriending, blocking, privating everything she could. The last thing she wanted was for Eric to find her. The last thing she needed was for him to pull her into his web of manipulation again. Not when she was still so vulnerable.

Luke: Your mom suggested you as a friend

Of course she had. Daisy rolled her eyes, her hesitation lessening.

Daisy: I don't need any friends right now. Thanks.

There was a long pause as the little speech bubble bounced up and down, then disappeared. Daisy watched the cursor on her laptop continue to spin, and she felt her heart beat faster. Did she really mean it?

Luke: I'm sorry. I didn't mean to overstep anything. We'll just be neighbors then.

Daisy stared at Luke's reply, her stomach sinking. No, that wasn't what she wanted. It was what she needed. She needed to do this on her own. She needed to forge her own path without someone dictating every move, belittling her along the way. She needed to learn to stand on her own two feet. She didn't need a friend right now, and she certainly didn't need a relationship on the heels of escaping a very manipulative one. Her thumbs hovered over the phone's keyboard, her breath coming short as she held back the words she couldn't quite figure out how to say.

Her laptop screen flashed white, and a message appeared in tiny text at the top.

We are experiencing higher than normal traffic. Your connection has timed out. Please try again later.

"Oh, it smells divine in here!" Mrs. Colton's voice

carried in from the front door.

Daisy closed her laptop. She hadn't even noticed her mother's car pull up.

"Are you okay?" Daisy asked, frantically flying down the hall. "They didn't send you home early, did they?"

"Home earl—no, Sunshine. Today's my day off." Several plastic grocery bags hung from Mrs. Colton's arms.

"Oh," Daisy said. She relieved her mother of a few bags, immediately rifling through them. "No ice cream?"

"I think you've had enough for a while," Mrs. Colton said, tapping Daisy gently on the end of her nose. "If you want more, you can get it yourself."

"It's fine," Daisy said, though her sunken shoulders couldn't hide her slight disappointment. "You're right, I have been eating a lot of it. It's comfort food for me. Eric didn't allow it in the house."

"He didn't allow ice cream in the house?" Mrs. Colton asked, lifting the lid of the crock-pot. She leaned over, taking in a deep breath.

"No sweets. He didn't want me to get fat. He said it would affect my tips at work, and we couldn't afford the hit to our income."

Mrs. Colton replaced the lid, her lips pursed. "I really, really don't like that boy."

"Yeah, me either," Daisy said, smiling. She replayed the words she'd spoken. They should have felt like ash in her mouth, but they didn't. The words fell from her lips as naturally as truth. Because it was the truth. A twisted version of the truth that Eric had made Daisy believe.

"So, when is this heavenly masterpiece of yours going to be ready?" Mrs. Colton asked, bringing Daisy from her introspection.

"It was Chef Andrew's recipe," Daisy corrected, "but not until seven."

"Alas!" Mrs. Colton threw an arm across her forehead, and Daisy giggled.

The last of the groceries were neatly put away—sans toilet paper and hand sanitizer, Daisy noted—and the lid to the crock-pot secured back in place, despite Mrs. Colton's attempts to sneak a taste of the sauce. After being shooed unceremoniously from the kitchen, Mrs. Colton dragged Daisy outside, tossing a pair of gardening gloves her way.

"You can paint flowers, but can you prune them, Missy?" she teased.

"I don't know. This old lady tried to teach me when I was little."

"Old lady, is it?"

Daisy shielded herself from the scattering of dirt her mother tossed at her, shrieking and laughing.

"It's such a beautiful day for March," Daisy mused. Slight breaks in the gray clouds overhead revealed a light blue sky. "I didn't realize how much I missed it."

"Missed what?"

"Home."

Mrs. Colton's understanding eyes washed over Daisy, before returning to her gardening. "I'm glad we could spend some time together," she said. "I've been so busy with work, and you've had to be on your own."

"Mom, I'm a big girl. I can take care of myself. It's okay."

"I know you can. That's not what—I meant, I really wanted to spend time with you while you were here."

"What do you mean?" Daisy asked, pulling at a particularly stubborn thistle weed.

Mrs. Colton wiped at the sweat that formed across her brow. "I'm not so naïve to think you're here to stay forever. Eventually, whatever chased you away from Arizona will resolve itself, or you'll find a new path and take off on that one. I've missed you, Daisy."

"I missed you too, Mom." Daisy squeezed her mother's hand, holding her gaze before returning to what some would call pruning. Daisy thought of it more as mass extermination. "Geez, Mom! When was the last time you tended the garden?"

"Before the snowfall."

"Mom, this is northwest Ohio. That could have been a week ago."

"Perhaps before the snowfall of last year."

The jingle of a dog collar signaled the approach of a jogger, and Daisy turned as Luke and Apollo approached. Luke had changed out of his uniform and into a pair of loose gym shorts and a Spiderman tank that stretched across his defined chest.

"Hello, Luke!" Mrs. Colton called.

Daisy quickly released her bottom lip from her teeth, but it was too late. Mrs. Colton winked at her, and Daisy blushed.

"Hello, Mrs. Colton. Miss Daisy," Luke replied, slowing to a stop and commanding Apollo to sit.

"How are you holding up, dear?" Mrs. Colton wiped her brow again, looking at Daisy from the corner of her eye.

Daisy leaned over the flowerbed, trying to ignore the rush that seemed to overtake her each time she looked at Luke.

"They've talked about running us double shifts. We're getting a lot of calls for heart attacks, but most turn out to be panic attacks."

"Oh, poor dears. And poor you! Why aren't you getting some rest?"

Apollo's collar jingled again as the dog shook from head to tail. "Fluffy Butt needed to burn off some energy."

Apollo barked as if in agreement, and Luke gave some slack in the dog's leash when Mrs. Colton held out a hand for pets. The dog's snuffling toward the older woman was short-lived, however, as he was far more interested in Daisy. He managed two licks to her face before Luke pulled him back.

"Apollo, no! We do not lick pretty girls!"

The dog huffed, sitting again at the man's feet.

"Don't you backtalk me," Luke scolded. "No licking

people without permission. We've covered this. Sorry about that."

Daisy didn't answer. Her heart had fluttered at Luke's words. She continued to wipe her face long after Apollo's slobber had been removed in an effort to hide… why was she blushing?

Mrs. Colton unsuccessfully hid a smile. "Well, make sure you get some rest. I'll send over some of Daisy's dinner tonight."

"No!" Daisy shouted before she could stop herself.

"Daisy! That's—"

"It's okay," Luke interjected. "I have plenty of leftovers. See you later, Mrs. Colton! Miss Daisy."

Luke and Apollo took off, the flush in Daisy's face subsiding.

"Daisy Lynn Colton, that was rude!"

"I'm sorry! I just meant—dinner's probably not going to be that good."

"Luke wouldn't have cared. Daisy, that man likes you!"

"No, he doesn't," Daisy said, though her voice held little conviction to support her words.

Mrs. Colton turned square to her daughter, hand on her hip. "So, it's like *that*, is it?"

"Like what?" Daisy tossed her gardening trowel into a clump of hostas, squaring up to her mother with her own hand on her hip and an identical purse to her lips.

"You like him too."

"No, I don't! I know what you're trying to do. Don't."

"What am I trying to do?"

Her lip threatening to shake, Daisy paused, but it wasn't enough to staunch the pain. "Mom, you have no idea what I've been through, the things Eric's done and said to me."

Mrs. Colton relaxed her stance. "You're right. I don't," she said, her voice soft. "But it must have been quite troubling for you to leave your friends and your job behind. I know how much you loved that job."

Hot tears ran down Daisy's cheeks as Eric's words struck again.

"You know those girls only like you because you get all the good tips, and you have to split them, right? Which is why you listened to me when I told you to do your makeup and hair. No one wants to look at an ugly waitress before eating, Daisy."

"I didn't leave any friends behind. I don't have any friends."

"That's not true."

"Isn't it?" Daisy's anger boiled to the surface. "None of them have even reached out to me!"

"Well, they've reached out to me," Mrs. Colton said, halting the retort that waited at the end of Daisy's tongue. "They were worried about you and didn't want to bother you."

"Whatever. I don't need any friends right now. I need to figure out how to do this on my own. Friends just stab you in the back, anyway." Daisy ripped out a clump she wasn't sure was weed or flower and threw it into the pile, not bothering to shake out the dirt first. The soil flew into the air, narrowly missing her mother.

"The people who stabbed you in the back were not your real friends, Daisy."

"You think I don't know that? You think I don't recognize the mistakes I made? You want to talk about all the trouble I was in? More like all the trouble I *allowed* myself to get in. You don't even know the half of it. Just—forget it." The tears had returned, leaving tracks through the bits of dirt that clung to Daisy's cheeks. "I'm going to get some ice cream."

A mask, gloves, and a pair of swimming goggles sat in the passenger seat as Daisy flew down Karis Road. In hindsight, the goggles might have been a little extreme, but that was Daisy! Never thinking things all the way through. How many ideas did Eric have to talk her out of? How many stupid plans had she made, only to be brought back down to reality again? No, her mother *didn't* know the half of it. Because more than half of it meant Daisy admitting how much she'd screwed up her own life. She wasn't ready to face those consequences yet.

"If it wasn't for me, you'd be homeless and living on the street. You know you can't do anything with an art degree. I don't know what you were even thinking."

"You're acting like I'm the bad guy here. I'm the one that's keeping a roof over our head and food on the table. Who pays for your cell phone? Who co-signed on a car for you?"

"I never said you were stupid. I said it was a mistake.

You're *the one who said you were stupid, so if that's what you want to think, I'm not stopping you."*

Dozens of conversations replayed in Daisy's mind in a matter of moments. And every feeling, every emotional response she'd pushed down seemed to break through the feeble barrier she'd created. The tears on her face were more than a physical response. They were the swallowed words she'd never spoken, the emotional bruises and scars she carried on her heart. Locked away, like a princess in a tower, so she could more easily believe the truth that Eric had fed her.

A black streak darted across the street. Daisy slammed on her brakes, smelling the burning rubber of the tires as the car jolted to a stop. She must have hit it. Whatever it was, she had to have hit it.

Her hands shook as she peeled them off her steering wheel. Daisy looked in her review mirror. There was nothing on the road. She scanned the area and gasped when her eyes fell on a little black kitten. It lay flat in the grass on the opposite side of the road, unmoving.

"Oh, God. Oh, no." She had hit it. There was no question. And if it was still alive...

Her body was sluggish to respond, but somehow, Daisy managed to put the car in park. She looked up, and the kitten was gone. If it had slunk off somewhere to die... She unbuckled her seat belt and reached for the door, hands still shaking like mad. Maybe she could still find it. Maybe she could take it to a vet. But the vets were all closed.

Daisy opened her door and shrieked. The little black kitten jumped into her lap, purring and rubbing against her stomach. It stepped over the gearshift and made itself comfortable atop the swimming goggles, still purring and kneading the seat.

"Oh, no. No, no, no. We're not doing this. If you're not hurt, then you can just move along."

Thoughts of that morning's news report replayed in Daisy's mind.

"Overseas, a couple's feline companion has been diagnosed with this dangerous virus," the reporter had said. "Once thought to only affect humans, scientists now wonder if this illness is zoonotic and if it can spread from cats to people."

Daisy lifted the kitten from the seat where it hung limply in her hands. It stretched as it passed in front of her, rubbing beneath her chin and purring louder.

"No. Don't even think about it." She dropped the kitten back on the street, and it immediately hopped into the car, this time curling up in her lap.

In the rearview mirror, Daisy saw another car approaching in the distance. With an aggravated sigh, she shut the door.

"Fine. But don't get too comfortable. This isn't permanent." As she put the car in drive, the kitten gave her arm a single lick and fell asleep.

The store was a sea of masks and empty shelves. Painter's tape had been hastily laid on the floor to encourage a minimum of six feet of distance between shoppers. Luckily, the ice cream freezers were decently stocked, as were the pet shelves. Fifteen minutes and over $100 later, Daisy made her way back to her car, arms loaded down with what she hoped were the correct cat essentials and seven pints of ice cream.

She glanced through the side window and saw the kitten sleeping on the passenger seat. She tiptoed to the trunk, quietly loading the bags inside. When she closed the trunk, she jumped. The kitten sat in the back window, staring up at her with wide, yellow eyes.

"Don't you move!" she demanded.

Daisy waved her finger, envisioning the ungrateful creature darting across the parking lot when she opened the door. But the kitten remained still when she climbed inside, even waiting until her door was closed before returning to the front seat.

"Well, at least you're an obedient little thing."

As Daisy pulled out of the parking lot, she found herself glancing at the kitten as she drove.

"I hope you're happy with yourself," she said.

The kitten licked its front leg.

"Enjoy it while it lasts, kid. I meant what I said. This isn't permanent. In fact, it's only for tonight, you hear me?"

The kitten moved on to grooming its stomach.

"I mean it. I'm calling the shelter tomorrow. Man, I

hope Mom doesn't kill me for this. Oh, and you better be okay with dogs, because there's a giant fluff ball that thinks he owns the place. I don't think his owner would much like it if he got his face all scratched up."

The kitten blinked at Daisy, then lifted its back leg in the air, continuing its bath.

"Then again, I guess it would serve them right for leaving an animal in the care of a blind moron. I mean, who doesn't notice when a car is parked in the driveway?"

The kitten mewed in response.

"I must be going insane. I'm talking to a cat."

It was silly, borderline lunatic, and yet somehow comforting. The kitten yawned, seeming satisfied with its grooming job, and settled into Daisy's lap again. As the car rumbled down the road, Daisy set a hand on the kitten. She felt the rumble of its purr reverberate through her body, and her shoulders relaxed.

The front yard was empty when Daisy pulled into the drive. Her mother must have moved on to pulling weeds in the backyard. All the better for Daisy.

She quietly carried the kitten inside, settling it in her room with the supplies she'd purchased. It darted under her bed, then poked its head out, covered in cobwebs. Daisy's lip curled in disgust. Had all that been under her bed? The wine ice cream she'd snatched on clearance was definitely in order for tonight. She opened her bedroom door and nearly ran headlong into her mother.

"Mom! Geez, you scared me!" Daisy cried, trying to close the door behind her before the kitten snuck out—or her mother saw the incriminating evidence before she explained.

"How much ice cream did you buy?" Mrs. Colton asked, her eyes glancing over Daisy's shoulder. "Wait, is that a litter box? Where did you get a cat?"

"Don't be mad—"

"I'm not mad, but how on earth—"

"It ran out in front of my car!" Daisy said, throwing her arms in the air, pumped and ready to defend her actions. "I almost hit the thing, and when I opened my door to check on it, it jumped inside! I tried to get it to leave but… it's just for tonight."

"Just tonight?"

Daisy crossed her arms. "I'm calling the shelter in the morning."

"I think all the animal shelters are closed down right now, Sunshine."

"What!"

The kitten popped out from behind Daisy's dresser, prancing over to the women and winding itself around their feet.

"Oh, it's so cute! Daisy, you have to keep it."

"No. I told it, it was just for tonight."

"You… told the cat."

"We had a conversation. Don't question it."

Mrs. Colton smirked, picking the kitten up and smushing it against her face.

"Anyway, how do you know the shelters are closed down?" Daisy asked. This was not the reaction she had prepared herself for.

"Luke told me."

Daisy rolled her eyes. Definitely not the way she planned for this conversation to go. At all. "Of course he did."

"He volunteers as a dog walker and sometimes a foster."

Great. Luke Richards was now charming, possibly liked movies and pop culture as much as Daisy—if his taste in shirts was to be believed—*and* he was good with animals.

"Of course he does." The man was practically a modern male version of a *Disney* princess.

The kitten struggled against Mrs. Colton's grip, and she set it down. Daisy watched it investigate the litter box, pawing at the contents before using it. At least she didn't have to worry about that.

"Daisy, listen to me just for a minute," Mrs. Colton said, her voice soft. She set a hand on Daisy's shoulder and sighed. "You were right. I don't understand what you've been through, and I'm here to listen whenever you're ready to tell me. But I see you fighting whatever this is between you and Luke."

"Mom—" Daisy stopped when Mrs. Colton held up her hand.

"As your mother, as someone who loves you more than anything and anyone in the world, I want to give you the permission you won't give yourself. Don't fight it, okay?"

"I don't know what you're talking about."

"I'm talking about how you like Luke, and he likes you. Just let it happen and see where it goes, okay?"

"You realize I've only been here for two days. I... I only had the urge to leave Arizona a week ago, and I'm still trying to process... all of it."

"You are a good person, Daisy," Mrs. Colton said, her voice remaining steady even as Daisy felt like breaking down again. "You deserve someone who sees that in you, and can reciprocate it."

Daisy sighed, blinking back the tears she felt threatening to fall again. "I'll try. It's just scary, you know? You learn how to read between the lines for one person, and then everything starts to sound like a lie."

The word fell from her lips, hanging in the air between them, but only Daisy seemed to notice. Lies. Giving a name to what Eric did to her only made her dependency on him seem all the more naïve. She told herself it was just a version of the truth she couldn't see herself, but she knew what it was all along. And she'd let herself become entrapped in it. She let herself become the martyr.

"Well, I'm your mother. I can't lie to you." Mrs. Colton kissed her daughter's brow. "It's in the handbook."

Daisy's tension fell away at her mother's loving gesture, and she smiled. "Oh, yeah? Two words. Santa

Claus. Two more. Easter Bunny. Oh, two *more*. Tooth Fairy."

"Yeah, well, that was in the handbook too. Now, what are you going to name your kitten?"

Daisy sighed. "Mom, I don't have time for a pet."

"Really? Because you seem to have enough time to declutter my kitchen."

"Well…" Daisy paused, struggling for an answer. "I don't even know if it's a girl or a boy."

"I'm sure we can look it up on the internet. Or ask Lu—"

"We are not asking Luke to look at my cat's genitals."

"See? I knew you'd come around."

Daisy pushed past her mother, marching back out to the car for the two bags of ice cream. "It's not staying," she called over her shoulder.

"We're not putting it back outside. If the shelters can't take it, *I'm* keeping it. Deal?"

"Fine," Daisy agreed, slamming her trunk closed. "But no names until we have to keep it."

day 8

Little paws and tiny claws pushed against Daisy's face. She opened her eyes and found the little black kitten staring back at her. It mewed, kneading her neck before settling in, its purrs melting her heart and still-groggy mind.

She grabbed her phone, careful not to disturb the kitten as she snapped a picture. The messy bun she'd worn to bed released strands of platinum blonde tendrils that framed her face. Daisy opened her photo editor, adding a filter and cropping the top of her head to hide the ash-blonde roots that were showing through.

I appear to be trapped, she captioned the picture on her social media page. She pressed Enter, and the kitten looked up at her, eyes half shut and a smug expression on its muzzle.

"You're still not staying," she reminded the cat. "I'll keep calling the shelters every few days until there's an opening."

Daisy set the kitten on the pillow beside her, now free from her cat paralysis prison. A shower, a bowl of cereal, and a bath for the kitten after it fell into its plate of canned food later, she opened her laptop again. She was determined to get the unemployment website to work for her. The kitten sauntered out of the room, shaking its back legs every few steps. It jumped into the bay window, basking in the sun and bathing the last of the damp patches.

Daisy's mouse cursor spun in a circle as she sat on hold with the local animal rescues again and again.

"Hi! Yes, I'm looking for a place to take a kitten. No? Oh, okay. Thanks."

"Hello. Uh... yes, it's me again. I'm still looking for—you're still closed? All right. Thank you."

"Hello, I'm looking for a rescue for a kitten I found. It's really small and you can have everything I bought for it already. No, no, I can't really keep it. Yes, I'm already on the three-week waiting list. Thanks."

We are experiencing higher than normal traffic. Your connection has timed out. Please try again later.

Daisy sighed, watching the kitten chase shadows of the birds that flew across the sunbeams. She reached for her phone and opened her social media app. Over a dozen notifications waited for her. The photo of her and the kitten had garnered several likes, and even a few comments.

"So cute!" said an old high school classmate.

"Aw!" her Aunt Jonie commented.

"Miss you, girl!" This one was from Mel, a waitress at *The Modern Plate*.

Daisy paused at the sight of Mel's name. Perhaps she was being too lax. The social media algorithms were always changing, and Eric was well-versed in digging up information. She stared at the photo a moment longer before deleting it and immediately double-checked her security settings.

The unemployment website timed out for the second time. Daisy closed her laptop, trying not to let her mind wander to every negative what-if scenario that all inevitably ended with Eric showing up on her doorstep.

With the last of her canvas now sitting in the parlor corner, she grabbed a yellowing sketchbook she'd unearthed from the kitchen table and joined the kitten in the window. Her sketch pencils were a bit dried out, but they still worked. The kitten yawned and stretched as Daisy settled in beside it, its shadow hunting now complete.

She set her pencil to paper, letting the gentle strokes of the graphite build from light to dark. It had been a long time since she'd done more than a doodle on the corner of a page. The muscles in her hand ached as she practiced holding the pencil in proper form for the first time in years.

The ping of Daisy's social media messages sounded from her pocket. She gave into the temptation, allowing her hand a slight reprieve from holding the pencil. She set aside the sketchpad and swiped at the message bubble.

A picture taken from across the street showed the kitten basking in the sun with Daisy snuggled into the nook of the window, pencil and paper in hand.

Luke: I thought you didn't need any friends.

Daisy: It's not mine. It ran in front of my car yesterday. I'm only keeping it until the shelters open.

Daisy scrolled up, looking at the picture again. Was that really what her profile looked like? She ran a finger down the bridge of her nose as another message popped up, forcing the picture out of sight as it jumped to the bottom of the conversation.

Luke: Are you okay? Is the kitten okay? It wasn't hurt? Do you want me to take a look?

Daisy: She's fine. Or he. I don't know what it is. But it's fine. It jumped into my car when I stopped.

She looked at the kitten sprawled on its back at her feet. The thing was more than fine.

Luke: It sounds like you have a cat.

Daisy: Like I said, it's not staying. Besides, I thought you were a paramedic, not a veterinarian...

Daisy smirked at her sharp response, anxiously awaiting Luke's counter banter.

Luke: How did you know I'm a paramedic?

Busted.

Daisy: My mom told me. And I saw your uniform when you came home from work last week.

Luke: So, you're talking about me to your mom?

Daisy's cheeks flushed. Totally busted. The kitten stretched again, snuggling into the side of Daisy's leg. She scratched its ears and stopped. She would not get attached. She looked across the road, searching the windows of Luke's house. If he was still watching, she wasn't going to give him any ammunition toward her about it.

Daisy: It's not like that.

Luke: Well, what is it like? I'd like to know where I stand in all this.

The thought of where she'd like Luke to be standing

at that moment bulldozed its way through Daisy's mind. She suppressed a shiver.

Daisy: It's nothing, and I don't have a cat, okay?

She watched the text bubble bounce for several long moments, a sinking feeling growing in the pit of her stomach. Perhaps her mother had been right. She *was* pushing Luke away, and though it was difficult to admit, she didn't want to.

Luke: I've worked with animals for a long time. I've volunteered with rescues and at shelters since I was a child. My family fostered a lot when I was a kid. Anyway, you can call it fate or God or a sixth sense on the animal's part, whatever you want. But I'm telling you, animals don't just mysteriously come to people like that without a reason. You've been chosen, Daisy. Con-cat-ulations!

Daisy: Con-cat-ulations? Really?

But she was smiling.

Luke: What? Don't appreciate my sense of humor?

Daisy: Oh, that was supposed to be a JOKE! I see.

She could never have bantered with Eric in this

way. He had lacked a distinct sense of humor, at least anything that wasn't bordering on condescending.

Luke: Admit it. It was funny.

Daisy: Let me know when you're planning on coming over next. I don't want an encounter between the kitten and Apollo going poorly.

Luke: Apollo loves cats, but understood, my lady.

A sparrow darted outside the bay window, drawing the kitten's attention, and it leapt at the glass, leaving streaky paw prints in its wake.

"I'll admit. You are cute," Daisy said. "I'll be right back. Don't move."

Between the stress of leaving—and the stress-eating of so much ice cream—Daisy's digestion had taken a turn for the worse. Her insides gurgled as she hurried to the bathroom, making it just in time. She reached for the switch for the fan, as her eyes fell on the near-empty toilet paper roll.

Oh, no.

Very carefully, Daisy checked beneath the sink and the storage shelf above the toilet. Nothing. Thank God she was still in the habit of bringing her phone to the bathroom. And after this, she made a mental note to invest in copious amounts of phone cleaner instead of breaking the habit. One had to make sacrifices in a pandemic, after all.

Daisy: Mom, where do you keep the toilet paper?

Daisy carefully pulled the few meager squares of toilet paper from the roll as she waited. She folded them in various ways, as if they would miraculously multiply.

Mom: Under the bathroom sink.

Daisy set the squares aside, typing an answer like her life depended on it.

Daisy: There isn't any there!

Mom: Then I guess we're out.

Daisy: WHAT?

This could not be happening right now.

Mom: You were at the store yesterday. You saw the state of the shelves. And with as much ice cream as you've been eating lately, I thought you'd be constipated for a week.

Daisy: You're not funny. Can you come home and bring me some napkins from a drive-through or

something?

Mom: I've already taken my break, Sunshine. I'm sneaking this conversation as it is. I'm sorry. Why don't you ask Luke?

An audible groan escaped Daisy. She could deal with fate, or God, or some unknown cosmic force bringing a cat into her life. She didn't know if she was prepared for whatever kept trying to bring that man closer into her life. A small toot escaped her. No, she was not prepared for something that close right now.

Daisy: No way. Absolutely not.

Mom: Then, I guess you'll just have to wait another four hours. Sorry, Sunshine. I have to go.

Daisy inhaled, leaned back, and would have screamed if a tiny black paw beneath the door hadn't distracted her.

I am not asking Luke for help.

She checked the cabinet beneath the sink once more. No, there definitely wasn't any toilet paper.

I am not asking Luke for help.

She spied a box of feminine supplies. Perhaps if she was careful... no, that wouldn't work. Daisy looked down at the blue and gray striped toe-socks she had pulled out of her dresser. The thought made her shudder.

Daisy: Hey, are you still home? I'm not bothering you from sleeping or anything, am I?

Luke: It's never a bother to hear from you. What's up? Is your kitten okay?

There was no easy way to do this.

Daisy: This is embarrassing, but I ran out of toilet paper. You wouldn't happen to have a spare roll by chance?

The chat application went silent. Not even the texting indicator danced below her last message. Daisy could just picture Luke laughing at her. She knew he'd never let her live this down. So much for giving herself permission to explore a relationship. This was about to kill any chances she might have had.

The texting indicator popped up, and Daisy sighed in relief. Relationship or no, she was still desperate for toilet paper.

Luke: The troops and I have discussed the state of our supplies and are willing to part with a roll. Meet you outside?

Thank goodness.

When the quarantine was first announced, Daisy had resisted the urge to panic-buy anything. Unless one considered buying seven pints of ice cream panic-buying. Perhaps she would judge her fellow shoppers a little less harshly now. She looked at the box of feminine supplies and wiggled her toes in the blue and gray striped toe-socks before replying.

Daisy: I… I'm kind of stuck at the moment, if you get my drift. Also, you can help yourself to some of the ice cream in the freezer. I don't think I'll be having any for a little while.

Luke: Say no more. I'm on my way.

Daisy blinked at her phone in shocked disbelief. A wave of… something… washed over her. Relief? In the back of her mind, she knew she'd been preparing for a fight, to defend herself from the jeers and teasing that should have come before any acquiescence. But it never came.

The front door opened, and the little paw beneath the door disappeared.

"Hello, little one," she heard Luke's distant voice.

As his footsteps drew closer, Daisy's rear released a nervous poot of gas. She fumbled for the switches. She had neglected to turn on the fan when she saw the state of her predicament. The thought of Luke being able to smell the disaster she'd unleashed in the bathroom was horrifying. His shadow appeared at the base of the door, then disappeared just as quickly. He *had* smelled it, Daisy was sure of it.

The footsteps faded, but not enough to reach the front door. Then she heard the freezer door open and shut. He'd actually taken her up on that. She shook her head, waiting for the sound of the door to open and shut again.

She jerked the door open and snatched the roll of toilet paper from the hall as her messaging app pinged.

Luke: Supplies delivered. Also, your kitten is a boy.

Daisy didn't bother attaching the roll to the holder. She wound the toilet paper around her hand and watched a green sticky note fall to the floor, landing with its message face up between her feet.

In exchange for one roll of toilet paper, Apollo would like to request a virtual dinner. What's that boy? Oh, he says he'll be on his best bark-havior.

Daisy smiled. She finished cleaning up, and even skipped her habitual second washing, reaching for her phone to type out a reply.

Daisy: Just friends.

Luke: Friday at 8?

Daisy: Okay.

Luke: Apollo says that's Woof-er-ful! See you then!

Daisy opened the bathroom door and found the kitten savaging a well-loved feather-wand Luke must have left. She noticed a few other toys scattered around the living room. None of them looked new, but clearly that didn't bother the kitten.

Her heart fluttered as she sank into the heather-gray sofa, unable to stop smiling. Luke Richards had asked her to dinner.

day 12

Pepper wishes you all a happy Fur-I-Day! Daisy captioned the picture of her and the kitten before posting it to her new social media account. She held Pepper next to her cheek, his glossy black fur tickling her face. She gave the kitten a final kiss on his nose and sat up in bed, setting Pepper at her feet. Wiggling her toes, she watched as the kitten pounced and nibbled at his prey. She giggled, scrunching her toes and pivoting on her heels as Pepper batted at the bug she'd painted on her big toenail the prior evening.

When it became more than clear that the local shelters were in no position to take the kitten, Daisy gave in to her mother's imploring remarks and pleading eyes. Mrs. Colton immediately called in a favor from a friend, and Pepper was given a mostly clean bill of health from a local veterinarian. A few doses of a parasite medication and he was good until his next booster shot.

Daisy headed toward the bathroom, Pepper following close behind. She'd forgotten how much she enjoyed having an animal companion. Eric wasn't an animal lover, or even an animal-tolerater. The kitten made himself comfortable in Daisy's discarded pajama top as she climbed into the shower.

Pepper's company, while a contributing factor to Daisy's more cheery mood of late, wasn't the only thing brightening her spirits. As the hot water poured over her, and the sounds of the kitten tussling with her buttons outside the shower curtain persisted, Daisy couldn't shake her excitement. Tonight was her virtual dinner with Luke. Well, with "Apollo," but she hoped the conversation would be a bit more than which brands of tennis balls flew the furthest.

It was almost two weeks since she'd left Eric. Two weeks and not a word. No phone calls or manipulative text messages. The silence had at first been terrifying. She'd learned how to handle Eric's outbursts. Silence, however, was like swimming in an ocean unable to see the bottom. What was he thinking? What was he planning? But that fear had slowly ebbed away as the days and weeks persisted without incident. In the quiet solitude of home, Daisy was formulating a plan. In her mind, she was building a new life after the quarantine ended. And maybe… just maybe… she could keep a little space for love in it as well.

It was already well into the afternoon. Daisy had fallen into a bad habit of sleeping in. Between the stress of the world-wide pandemic and leaving Eric, it was a small slice of freedom and control she was only just beginning to let go. She settled onto the sofa, her father's afghan wrapped around her legs, and Pepper purring in her lap, and dialed the number for Arizona's unemployment office.

"We are experiencing a higher than normal call volume. Your call is important to us. Please stay on the line, and your call will be answered by the next available representative. You are caller… 27… in line."

Daisy set the phone beside her, occupying herself with her sketchbook once again as the hold music repeated in a constant loop, occasionally interjected by an automated voice.

The pencil glided across the paper, leaving traces in varying shades of gray as Daisy increased and decreased her pressure. After forty-five minutes, she held up a picture of Apollo and squinted.

"… You are caller… 3… in line."

She supposed the sketch wasn't terrible. She ripped the paper from the pad, shrugging off the dog's goofy face as a practice run. She set the pencil to paper again, her hand following the image she saw in her mind's eye. Stroke by stroke, the outlines of an eye came into being, complete with a wisp of dark brown hair falling across it.

The hold music stuttered, and a polite woman's voice came through. "Thank you for holding. This is Yolanda. To whom do I have the pleasure of speaking with today?"

Daisy fumbled to take the call off speakerphone. "Daisy Colton," she managed to get out.

"Hello, Miss Colton. And how are you doing today?"

"I'm… really well today. Thank you," Daisy said, the pencil in her hand continuing to trace lines across the sketchpad.

"That's wonderful to hear! It's a crazy time out there. What can I help you with today?"

"I need to file for unemployment."

Daisy heard the tapping of computer keys in the background.

"Of course. I can help you with that. Let me give you my direct extension number. In case the call drops, or if you need anything else after we're finished."

Daisy continued to draw as Yolanda asked her a series of questions. It calmed her and kept both her mind and heart from racing. Eric always handled their finances. Calls to the insurance companies, utility offices, even the pharmacy. They were all Eric's domain.

"I don't want you to make a mistake," he would say. *"I don't want you to feel bad because I'd have to go back and fix it. It's just better if I do it from the start."*

But there were no mistakes. No accidental misspeakings that would make government agents show up at her door, or court orders dragging her before a judge. It took all of fifteen minutes and Daisy's application for unemployment was filed. Yolanda confirmed Daisy had her extension number and ended the call.

Daisy looked at the blank phone in her hand, then at Pepper.

"Well, then," she said and shrugged.

Pepper reached a paw toward the end of her pencil, and she booped him on the nose with her eraser. She smiled and looked down at the sketch she'd been working on. Luke's face stared back at her, complete with his coy smile and 90s boy band haircut.

Her face fell as Pepper grappled the pencil from her hand. She didn't remember drawing Luke. A face, yes, but there was no denying it was Luke Richards that looked back at her from that yellowing page. She tore the page from the book, crumpling it up and burying it deep in the trash can. It was the last thing she wanted her mother to see—even if it was a near-perfect sketch.

She returned to the sofa, taking the pencil from Pepper before he chewed the eraser off. She'd admit she had a crush on Luke, but was this taking it a step too far? Was she low-key obsessing, or was this how love worked? A constant nudge at the edge of the mind, never ceasing, and ever-growing.

Daisy stroked the kitten's silky coat, her attentions preoccupied. Love didn't happen in real life like in the movies and books she longed to escape in. She knew that. Was it so wrong to want the fairy tale, even if she knew it didn't exist?

The sun moved across the sky and behind a tree. The shadows of fresh spring leaves danced across the floor, and Pepper jumped down to investigate. He pounced at the pattern spread across the floor, not grasping they weren't really there. They weren't real leaves. The shadows shifted as a gust of March wind waved the tree branch in a wild dance. Pepper ran in circles after the shadows.

It didn't matter that they weren't real. It didn't matter the shadows were but an illusion of leaves. The illusion made the game more fun, giving the kitten a chance to play the hunter without the risk of being hurt.

Daisy set her pencil to the sketchpad again, realizing the muscles in her hand didn't ache like they had a week ago. Her days of practicing had paid off. Her muscle-memory and strength had returned. The graphite glided across the page as the kitten continued to pounce at the shadows on the living room floor.

"Why was there a frozen pizza and a bottle of wine on the doorstep?" Mrs. Colton called down the hall.

Daisy emerged from the bathroom, her hair piled on top of her head. "That's for me," she said, taking the items from her mother and wiping them with the disinfectant wipes that now permanently lived by the front door.

"Oh?" Mrs. Colton raised an eyebrow, hanging her purse on the hook by the door. She accepted a wipe from Daisy, quickly sweeping it across her hands and exterior of the purse.

"It's nothing. I'm having a virtual dinner with a friend."

"I see."

Daisy ignored Mrs. Colton's astute tone. She intentionally had not told her mother about the virtual dinner with Luke.

"You were the one who said I should make friends

in the first place."

"I did indeed. This friend wouldn't happen to have a big, fluffy dog by chance."

Daisy didn't answer. She set the oven to preheat and returned to the bathroom.

This isn't a date, she told herself. *It's just a virtual dinner. With a friend.*

She stared at herself in the mirror, debating whether to put on makeup. Though she'd spent the last ten years believing people would be nicer to her if she dolled up, Luke had already seen her without it. A few times, in fact. She pulled her hair out of its messy bun, fingering the ash-blonde roots that poked through her dyed platinum-blonde locks. Another of Eric's suggestions. It was the color of all the Hollywood "it" girls.

She brushed out the tangles and opted for a bit of mascara and lipstick. She could use the filter on her camera to smooth out any other imperfections. After all, it wasn't a date.

"Your pizza's ready!" Mrs. Colton called down the hall.

Daisy looked at the time on her phone, eyes wide as she realized she'd spent over a half-hour fiddling around with her appearance. She flicked off the lights and bustled down the hall. Mrs. Colton held up a plate as she rounded the corner to the kitchen, preloaded with three slices of pizza, and a fresh wine glass.

"The bottle's a twist-off. I already checked." Mrs. Colton winked. "Enjoy your date."

"It's not a date!" Daisy yelled at her mother's retreating back. It wasn't.

Daisy deposited the wine and pizza on her dresser. Pepper paced before the chest of drawers, his eyes fixated on the plate, as he tried to figure out how to steal a slice.

"Don't even think about it, you little monster," Daisy as she pulled out her laptop.

She set the machine on her nightstand and checked the camera angle. Double chins. She pulled out her collection of Madeleine L'Engle books, stacking them together and lifting her laptop higher. A shadow appeared beneath her chin, slimming her jawline. Perfect. Now to deal with Orlando.

Daisy checked her phone again. 7:58 PM. Luke would call at any moment. She grabbed a shawl, draping it across the collage of magazine clippings behind her, and tacking them in place with pushpins from the corkboard. It would have to do. She rescued her dinner from Pepper's musings and shooed the kitten out of the room as a video chat notification popped up on her social media.

"It's not a date," Daisy told herself one last time, and with a cleansing breath, answered the call.

Apollo sat before the camera, wearing a bowtie on his collar. The fur on his ears and neck was fluffier and combed out. Even the whites on his coat popped more. Did Luke give him a bath?

"Hello, neighbor! Thanks for meeting me tonight!"

came Luke's voice off-camera.

Daisy laughed and poured the wine into the glass her mother had given her, noting for the first time how large it was.

"It's been awfully strange not having any dogs to play with. I'm glad I got to meet you!"

"I'm glad I met you too, Apollo."

"Apollo, bow," Luke whispered his command. The dog rested his head on his paws, eyes fixated on where Luke must have been standing behind the screen.

"I came from the Wood County Animal Shelter. Where are you from?" the cartoonish voice continued.

Before Daisy could answer, Pepper leapt onto her lap. Apollo barked in excitement, jumping onto the table and knocking the screen over. Luke cried out as Daisy watched the screen tumble end over end. It landed face-up on the floor, directly beneath where Luke stood in a pair of Batman underwear.

Daisy gasped, almost inhaling her wine. She roared with laughter, not caring that the kitten had somehow pushed its way back into her room and was now stealing a piece of sausage from her pizza. Luke picked up the device, ending the call instantly.

Concern washed over Daisy. She set her giant glass of wine on the nightstand as Pepper returned to her lap, looking for another treat. She shouldn't have laughed. She should have secured her bedroom door. She stared at the blank screen before her. Once again, Daisy had made a mistake. Her conversation with Yolanda earlier must have been an accident. She chugged half the glass of wine in one go. There went any chance she had.

The video chat notification popped up again. The now half-empty glass of wine teetered as Daisy hurried to answer, thankful she'd polished off a good portion of it before it ended up on her laptop.

This time, it was Luke who sat before the camera. He wore a sleek Batman tie, a button-down shirt, and a sheen of embarrassment.

"I am really, *really* sorry about that," he said.

Daisy couldn't hide her smile, though it was more out of relief than anything at this point. "I usually like to get to know my friends a bit better first, but I suppose it's good to know you're a boxers over briefs kind of guy."

Luke leaned forward, burying his face in his hands. "If it's any consolation, I am wearing pants now."

"It's okay. I haven't laughed like that in… well, it's been a long time."

Luke sat straighter, raising his own wineglass at the screen. "To boxers and furry companions, and to finding long-lost laughter."

Daisy raised her glass as well, taking another hearty drink. She was already beginning to feel the effects of her previous self-pity guzzle.

"I hope I got you the right kind of pizza. I never asked if you were vegetarian or anything."

"It doesn't have pineapple or anchovies, so I'm

good," said Daisy, taking a dainty bite. It was difficult to eat pizza like a lady, but she was determined to try.

"Oh, no. You're one of those?" Luke said, his eyes widening.

Daisy swallowed her piece, wiping her face with a paper towel with unnecessary veracity. "One of what?"

"A pineapple pizza snob."

Daisy set the paper towel in her lap. "No, I just don't think fruit belongs on savory pizza."

Luke's smug smile returned. "Ah, but tomatoes are a fruit."

"Yes, but… but…" She sighed in defeat.

Luke lifted his pizza for another bite, and Daisy noted there were, in fact, copious amounts of pineapple on it.

"So, where did you come from?" he asked.

"I lived in Erie River most of my life. I moved to Arizona for college."

Luke took another bite, a chunk of pineapple bouncing off his Batman tie and disappearing below the camera. "Wow, that's like another world."

"It is," Daisy admitted, and heard Apollo grunt somewhere off-camera.

"Did you enjoy it?"

Daisy paused. She took another bite, chewing slowly as she thought. "I don't know."

"You don't know if you enjoyed Arizona?"

"It's complicated."

Luke set his pizza on his plate, holding up two

grease-laden hands. "Say no more. What about college, or a job?"

Another sip of wine slid down Daisy's throat. She chased it with another for good measure. No matter how many questions she'd tried to prepare herself for, talking about her recent past was still awkward.

"I think I should get to know something about you," she said, hoping to dodge any more uncomfortable questions.

"Fair enough, but you already know I wear Batman boxers. There can't be anything more personal you could know."

Daisy narrowed her eyes, a smile pulling at the corners of her lips. "That sounds like a challenge."

Luke chewed and swallowed the last of his crust before replying, "Do you want it to be a challenge?"

Daisy polished off her first glass of wine, pouring herself a second. "I'll take it easy on you to start."

"Well, thank Heaven for that." Luke grinned, finishing his own glass and pouring another.

"Why did you become a paramedic?"

"To help people. I like the challenge of every situation being different and being there for people when they need someone the most."

"What about now, though? With everything going on?"

Luke sighed, his playful features growing more serious. "It's scary, I won't lie. There's a massive shortage of personal protective gear. Masks especially."

Daisy nodded. "The whole thing has me terrified. I feel like I'm in a constant state of panic, if I'm honest."

"You're not alone," Luke assured her.

"The only reason I went to the store the day I found Pepper was because I was angry."

"So, you named the kitten?" Luke gave her a knowing wink.

Daisy blushed, though it was difficult to tell through the rosiness the wine gave her cheeks.

"You know that makes it official, right?"

"Ok, fine, you were right," Daisy said.

"There's nothing wrong with changing your mind. Your kitten is very sweet. I think he'll be a nice companion for you."

"Thanks. I think." She wasn't sure how she felt about a complete stranger knowing her better than she knew herself.

"So, do I get to ask you a question now?"

"I suppose it's only fair. Ask away."

He paused, setting his now empty plate on the floor. "What's your favorite color?"

"That's it?"

Luke shrugged. "You went easy on me to start."

"Ok, then I'd have to say mint green."

"Mint green That's very specific. Kind of like the ice cream you love so much." He winked. "Thanks for the tub, by the way. I'm enjoying it."

"You're welcome. And I have to be specific with colors. I'm an artist, remember?"

"Do you have a particular... I don't know art stuff. Like, a specific kind of art that you enjoy the most?"

"Nope, it's my turn."

"All right, then. But I want to know when this challenge comes in."

"Is that so?" Daisy leaned toward the camera. "Well, Mr. Batman Butt, here is the ultimate question. The one that tests the courage of men, forsaking friends and either making or breaking all bonds of fellowship."

Luke gave a knowing smirk.

"Now's your chance to back out." Daisy took another sip, not realizing how much of the wine she'd drank yet again. But it was making her bold.

"No way. I am all in. Any woman who can quote *The Lord of the Rings* to me is worth it. So, shoot."

Daisy paused for dramatic effect, making a show of setting down her wineglass and staring directly into the camera.

"Star Wars or Star Trek?"

Luke leaned closer to the screen. "Both."

"You can't choose both!" Daisy cried, making Pepper jump awake from where he had settled at the end of her bed.

"Why not?"

"Because that's cheating."

"No, it's not. They are two very different kinds of stories."

"Oh, really?" Daisy crossed her arms, ignoring the tussles of the kitten behind her.

"Yes. Star Trek is about pushing boundaries, expanding your thoughts on not just science but life and humanity. It's about exploring that gray area between right and wrong. Star Wars is an action-adventure space opera about good vs evil. Clear lines between who and what is right and wrong."

Daisy sat back, a smirk spreading across her face. "You know the biggest travesty? You just admitted you're a geek."

Luke leaned back as well, lifting his wineglass. "Oh no. You already did that when you forgot to cover up Orlando Bloom as Legolas behind you," he said, taking another drink.

Daisy whipped around. One of the pushpins had given way as Pepper pounced and played with a tassel at the end of the shawl.

"Pepper!" Daisy cried. Startled, the kitten leapt away, but the shawl was already caught on one of his claws. The more Daisy tried to reach for the kitten, the further it ran, taking the shawl with it and revealing Daisy's old paper shrine to her childhood crush in all its majesty.

Luke cackled with laughter.

"It's not funny!" Daisy scolded, though she couldn't hide her own smile.

"Maybe not," said Luke, "but it's adorable."

"And what do you have on your wall, Batman Butt?"

"Is that my nickname now? Because I had a lot worse ones when I was in school."

"Yes, that is your name now. I will only address you as Mr. Batman Butt from now on." Daisy gave up on trying to reattach the shawl over the collage. He'd seen it now, anyway.

"Okay then, Mrs. Bloom," Luke shot back with a grin. "So, have you only seen the movies, or have you read the books too?"

"Read the books, of course. My dad started reading them to me at bedtime when I was little."

"Mr. Colton was a wonderful man. I miss him."

"Yeah, he was my best friend when I was growing up." And he never much cared for Eric. Daisy should have listened to him.

"What's your favorite book?"

"I think it's my turn to ask *you* a question," Daisy said, forcing her attentions back to the conversation. She'd spent enough time down the depressive black hole that was Eric.

"As you wish, my lady."

"Well? What's on your wall?"

Luke picked up the camera, panning it to the room behind him. "Absolutely nothing," he said laughing. "I'm in the process of tearing down the wallpaper my aunt installed when I was, like, five."

"I know an artist who could paint a Batman mural on there for you."

"Yeah? That'd be awesome!"

"How about after this quarantine is over?"

"Deal." Luke returned his camera to its previous

position, but not before Daisy saw he was, indeed, wearing pants.

"Okay, my turn," Daisy said. "Where did you go to college?"

"Because I'm a dog walker, you don't think I went to college?" Luke sat straighter, his face falling into disappointment.

"What? No, that has nothing to do with it," Daisy said, worry flooding her face.

Luke chuckled, his face lighting up with a grin. "I know what you meant. I graduated from Kent State."

"Kent State? In Ohio?"

"Yeah, well, they had the program I wanted."

"Dog walking 101?" she teased.

"Actually, no. That happened a bit on accident."

Daisy shifted on her bed, and Pepper crawled into her lap. "Yeah, so how exactly does a paramedic just happen to become a dog walker?" She stroked the kitten's velvety fur, feeling the low rumble of his purr.

"I was walking Apollo one day and someone asked if I would mind walking her dog and she said she'd pay me. Then another neighbor saw me, and they asked. Before I knew it, I was walking five dogs every other day. But because of the pandemic, I just walk Apollo now."

"Or bring him over for a play date?"

"Yeah. Well, it was supposed to be more than just him. But now that everyone is home, they can walk their own dogs. So, it's just Apollo."

"Don't you have your own yard?"

"It's not very big. I bought this house from my aunt a few years ago. Apollo was just a puppy then, and your mom invited me to use her yard anytime I wanted."

Daisy nodded again, setting her own empty plate aside for Pepper. "That sounds like Mom. She loves animals."

"Besides, if I hadn't, I never would have met you. At least not for a while." Luke leaned down to where Daisy assumed Apollo lay on the floor. "What's that boy?"

Apollo's head appeared at the bottom of the screen.

"That would have been a tragedy!" Luke said in his Apollo-voice.

"You're not funny," Daisy said, stifling a laugh.

"I can hear you giggling behind your hand."

"I do not giggle," she scoffed

"If you say so, Mrs. Bloom."

Their conversation spanned over three hours until the wine sat forgotten, and Daisy's sides hurt from laughing. There was no topic unexplored. Movies, books, animals, and the odd food reference for good measure. It was only Apollo's sharp bark, and Pepper startling at the noise that drew their conversation to a close.

"I hate to do this, but Apollo needs to go out, and I need to go to bed."

Daisy checked the time on her phone. "Yeah, I should try to start a proper routine. I've been sleeping in too much."

"I had a really great time, Daisy," Luke said, his voice dropping to a gentle sincerity.

"Yeah, me too," Daisy said, pulling her hair over her shoulder.

"Would... would you want to do this again?"

"I don't know. Are you bringing pants next time?"

"Only if you bring Orlando."

"Aye, that I can do," Daisy replied in her best Gimli voice.

Luke smiled, and Daisy was glad he'd recognized the reference.

"Goodnight, Daisy."

"Goodnight."

Daisy closed her laptop. She flopped back on the bed, staring at the ceiling like a love-struck teenager. At least her mood matched the décor of the room now. So, this was what a first date was like. She and Eric never had many date nights. There was never the money to celebrate in that way.

Her body felt light, and her head still whirled from the effects of the alcohol. At least Daisy assumed it was the entire bottle of wine she'd drunk. She bit her lip, wondering if it might be something more.

She rolled over, reaching for her phone. Mel had recently accepted her friend request on her new social media account. Mel seemed to have a new boyfriend every few months. She'd know, and it wasn't too late yet in Arizona.

Before Daisy could load her contacts, a text message flashed across the screen, and Daisy's heart sank.

Eric: Hey

Eric: I forgive you, you know. You don't think clearly when you get paranoid. I get it.

Daisy watched, frozen with fear, as the text messages slowly trickled in. Each one like a stab to her heart, killing any feelings that remained from her date with Luke. Even Pepper's resumed purring couldn't ease the tension that was growing inside her. She felt a tear slide down her cheek, and she wiped it away at the sound of the knock on her door.

Mrs. Colton peeked in, her smile quickly falling. "I was going to ask how things went tonight, but it doesn't look good. What happened?"

Daisy swallowed, somehow finding her voice. "No, my date with Luke was great. It's… Eric texted me."

Mrs. Colton pushed the door open the rest of the way. "Do you want to talk about it?"

The rapid ping of her text notification finally ceased,

and Daisy's phone went silent. There were over a dozen texts, but she couldn't bring herself to read them all. She looked at the blank screen, hands trembling.

"Daisy, I'm here. Even if you don't want to talk, you're not alone."

The seconds ticked by as Daisy felt her vision closing in around her, her mother's words the only thing breaking through the darkness that pulled her down further and further. That was why she had left. That was why she could no longer stay in Arizona. Because even if she showed up on Mel or Chef Andrew's doorstep, Eric would have found her. He'd have dragged her back to her cage, and she would have willingly succumbed. It's all she'd known for so long. Isolation.

Daisy moved over on the bed, making a space for her mother to sit. Mrs. Colton crossed the room in three strides, sitting in the proffered space. She took Daisy's hand, giving it a gentle squeeze, but remained silent.

"Did you know I wanted to go to Kent State for my art degree?" Daisy asked.

"I knew it was on your list, why?"

Daisy took a sip from her wineglass, the only drink she had available to quench her tight throat. "It was Eric's idea to move to Arizona. He said there were more opportunities out there. But, when I graduated, I couldn't find any work."

Step one, she thought, *isolate the subject.*

"Why didn't you move back here, Sunshine?" Mrs.

Colton lifted a hand as if to brush Daisy's hair back. She hesitated when she saw Daisy pull instinctively away and returned her hand to her lap.

"It wasn't that easy, Mom." Daisy shook her head.

Step two, make the subject dependent.

"I... I had a debit card and access to the bank accounts, but... I don't know why I never thought to regularly check the balance or ask about the monthly bills. You and Papa, you... I know about household accounting and budgeting. I mean, I thought I did, but Eric made it seem so complicated. I started to think I couldn't do it."

Daisy continued to stare at her mother's hands, holding tight to her own. She couldn't look away. She needed something to ground her. If she looked at her mother, what little strength she held might disappear. She did, however, hear her mother sniffle. She watched one of her mother's hands disappear, likely to brush away a tear, before returning to cover Daisy's hand again.

"And your friends? You didn't say anything to them?"

"I didn't have any friends, Mom. At least, he... he made me believe I didn't. He was the only one I had." Daisy took a deep breath. "I know it sounds crazy. Like, I knew it was all happening and I just let my world fall apart around me. But it was slow. It didn't happen all at once, you know? And, like I said, he was all I had, so I believed him."

No more tears had fallen since she began. Daisy finally looked up and saw she didn't need to. The pain she felt inside, every tear that should have rolled down her cheeks, was written on her mother's face.

"Mel tried to tell me. She really was my friend, and I feel... I feel terrible for not seeing it. Not reciprocating it. She told me it was gaslighting 101."

Step three, make the subject believe the narrative that you control.

"I had a moment of clarity, I guess. Maybe the fear of the pandemic made me aware of my fear of him, I don't know. Anyway, I made a plan, and I got out of there as fast as I could. I knew I had to act, or I'd chicken out."

"I'm sorry I didn't call you. I'm sorry I didn't see this."

"This isn't your fault, Mom. It's mi—"

"No! Don't you dare say it. Don't say the words he fed to you, Daisy. This is *not* your fault."

Daisy looked away and nodded. "Why is it so easy to believe all the bad things people say about you?"

"Because you're a good person, Daisy. And that... *boy*... he preyed on that goodness."

"The reason I didn't call," Daisy said, squeezing her mother's hand, "is because I didn't want to let you and Papa down. I thought I was a failure. I couldn't face you guys. I couldn't let you see your only child had wasted their life. I... I was ashamed."

This time, Daisy let her mother touch her cheek.

"You were never a failure to us, Daisy. We were prouder of you than you could ever know. I am still proud of you. So proud."

"I know that now. But it doesn't matter. Papa's gone, and the prime of my life is over."

"That's not true, Daisy," Mrs. Colton sat straight, cupping Daisy's chin in her hand.

"Mom, no one will want me anymore. I'm like that stupid coffee maker. Used up and broken beyond repair. Damaged goods."

"Daisy Lynn, you are *not* damaged goods. And the best years of your life are just getting started. You're home now. You're home, and safe, and you can start over. A man like Luke would never treat you that way." Mrs. Colton stood from the bed. "Stay there a moment."

Daisy watched her go, feeling the cold air in the empty space she had taken up before. Her footsteps padded back down the hall, and Mrs. Colton returned holding a picture frame. She sat on the bed again and handed Daisy the sketch she had done of Apollo.

"Luke would love this. Give him a chance, Daisy. Let him show you what love is supposed to be. I heard it in your voice not long ago. You were happy with him, Daisy."

"Mom, this isn't very good. I was just playing around—"

"Is that you or Eric talking?" Mrs. Colton raised a stern eyebrow, and Daisy smiled in understanding.

"Daisy, gifts from the heart aren't meant to be perfect. Tonight, think about the fun you had with Luke. We can deal with Eric in the morning."

"We?" Daisy asked, her voice catching.

"You're not doing this alone anymore." Mrs. Colton kissed Daisy's forehead and shut the bedroom door behind her.

day 13

With hands shaking, Daisy scribbled a message on a scrap piece of paper and folded it in half. The world was gray and wet, and though the sun had risen several hours prior, it was still too early for Daisy. She was beginning to second guess her commitment to getting in a better sleep routine.

She tucked the note and the framed picture of Apollo in Luke's mailbox, waving at the dog when he popped up over the couch by the front window as she approached. She'd hoped to quietly scuttle back across the street, but Apollo yipped and whined at her when she turned to leave. Daisy was sure she'd seen her neighbor, Mrs. Frothman's curtain move. So much for subtlety. At least Luke had already left for work.

Pepper greeted her at the door, meowing and demanding more breakfast. Daisy heard her mother turn on the shower as she pulled a skillet from the cupboard. She found an assortment of breakfast supplies and got to work, dodging the willful kitten at her feet.

Despite Eric's continued texts and phone calls throughout the night, Daisy was determined to feel happy. Her dinner with Luke had gone better than she could have imagined. Even if she didn't fully understand why, or how, or any of the feelings she was experiencing, she was ready to explore wherever that path would take her.

Eric's texts went unanswered and unheeded. She and her mother would deal with them later, because she didn't have to have all the answers right now. Answers for what to do about Eric, or the answers for how she felt about Luke and where she saw her friendship with him going. At least that's what she told herself, because it was easier than spiraling down a well of depression and anxiety again.

Mrs. Colton emerged from the bathroom, her hair twisted up in a towel as Daisy placed a freshly cooked egg in Pepper's food dish.

"Spoiling him already, I see," her mother said, taking a seat at the kitchen table Daisy had cleared off earlier.

"It was one I burned on accident. Here, before your pancakes get cold. Your eggs will be up in a minute." Daisy handed her a plate of Mickey Mouse shaped pancakes, complete with blueberry eyes and whipped cream smile.

Mrs. Colton chuckled and slathered the golden pancakes in butter. "You're in a good mood."

Daisy smiled, setting a plate of bacon on the table. "I am, yeah."

"So, tell me about your date."

Daisy bit her lip, fighting back the wide grin that threatened to contort her face. "It was… good. We have a lot of things in common, actually."

Mrs. Colton nodded. "I know."

"You know?" Daisy asked, joining her mother at the table with her own plate and several unburned eggs.

"He reminded your Papa and I a lot of you," Mrs. Colton said, cutting into her eggs. "He loves books and movies like you did when you were a kid. I'll admit, I kind of adopted him after you left. His mother passed away in a nasty house fire about six months after you moved out. He stayed with his aunt, Miss Dane, across the street. You remember Miss Dane. Anyway, she sold him the house a year ago."

"I guess that explains the Batman underwear," Daisy muttered, taking a bite of bacon and staring out the kitchen window to the garden beyond.

Mrs. Colton choked on her coffee, the dribbles barely missing her work shirt. "Excuse me?"

Daisy smiled, recalling the incident. "His camera fell, and he wasn't wearing any pants. He was wearing a pair of Batman-themed boxers, though."

"Thank Heaven," Mrs. Colton placed a hand on her heart. "You don't want to know what your poor mother was thinking you meant."

Daisy laughed through a mouthful of pancake.

"I know what you were thinking." It was probably something quite similar to what Daisy had been thinking as well. "I didn't know his mom died. I guess it also explains why he became a paramedic."

"Next time listen to your mother. I might be old, but I think I know when someone would get along with the person I birthed."

Daisy rolled her eyes. "Okay, Mom."

It wasn't that she couldn't admit when her mother was right. Mrs. Colton was a typical extrovert, able to read people almost as well as a trained psychologist. It was easy to admit her mother had been right about Luke. What wasn't easy was admitting to herself what she felt about him.

"What are your plans today?" Mrs. Colton asked, finishing the last of her breakfast.

"I think I'm going to paint my room."

"Ooh, nice."

Daisy shrugged, pushing her own empty plate away. "Eh, I have an idea in mind."

"As long as it's not a pair of Batman boxers, do whatever you want, Sunshine."

Blushing, Daisy stood, picking up the empty plates and dodging Pepper's attempts to trip her. "No, it's not a pair of boxers, Mom."

"Well, I can't wait to see it. I need to get going, Sunshine." She managed a kiss to Daisy's cheek, barely missing the kitten bounding around their feet. "Have a good day."

Daisy watched her leave, looking at her notifications and the six unread messages from Eric. No. She was not going there. Not alone. Perhaps never. She set the empty plates of eggs and bacon on the floor for Pepper to lick first, and began washing up, visions of hazel eyes and a muscular body trapped beneath a Batman costume playing in her mind's eye.

Deemed an unessential business, most of the art supply stores were closed. Daisy rummaged through her mother's basement, hoping to find it in a similar state to the kitchen. To her delight, a dozen half-gallon cans of paint lay beneath a pile of scrap wood in the corner. The remnants of a project she and her father had worked on together when she was a high school senior. Now, they would breathe new life into her and her room again.

She lugged the paint cans to the bedroom and covered her bed with a plastic tarp. Dipping a brush into a can of Payne's Gray paint, she sketched the outline of the picture in her mind. A garden of flowers—foxglove, daffodils, and daisies—poked out amongst a snow-scattered field. No matter how harsh the winters, or deep the frost, the first spring flowers were always guaranteed. They would always weather whatever life threw at them.

Pepper lay in the doorway, watching the brushstrokes glide back and forth over the wall.

"Don't even think about getting into these paints," Daisy chided. "The last thing we both want is to give you a bath."

The little kitten threw his back leg in the air and began grooming as if to let Daisy know exactly what he thought about baths.

Daisy pursed her lips, returning to her work with an audible huff. Stroke by stroke, the painting came to life. The messages from Eric lay forgotten, and Daisy found herself checking her phone not in fear, but in anticipation of Luke receiving her gift. Some fear existed, she had to admit. Fear of rejection. Fear of judgement. The fear that he'd see her work as Eric had, and the haunting words that replayed in her mind from years' past spilled from Luke's lips. She pushed the thoughts away, brushing the paint across her wall twice as fast as she had before.

It was late afternoon when the ringtone she'd assigned for Luke went off. Adam West's Batman theme reverberated through the room, and Daisy couldn't clean the paint off her hands fast enough. She reached for her phone and swiped at the notification.

Luke: Thank you for the picture! You really captured Apollo's goofiness. The tongue hanging out the side of his mouth was perfect!

Daisy released a sigh, a smile spreading across her face as she typed her reply.

Daisy: I was just playing around. It was actually

Mom's idea to give it to you. But I'm glad you liked it.

Luke: If this is you just playing around, I can't wait to see your work when you are serious.

She tucked a strand of hair behind her ear.

"You know your work isn't really that good," came Eric's words. She shook her head, pushing them away. Those were his opinions, not hers. And they clearly weren't Luke's either. She hoped.

Daisy: Thanks. Maybe I'll do one of you next time.

Luke: Come join me for a walk tomorrow with Apollo?

The words of a hundred news anchors, journalists, even opinionated social media trolls flooded Daisy's mind. But she wanted to see him again. Their dinner the night before was a moment in her life she'd never forget. A moment she had connected with someone in a way she never had before. But she also wanted to live to the end of this pandemic.

Daisy: I don't know if that's safe. Social distancing and all.

She pressed Enter, immediately regretting her

words. Each second that ticked by without seeing the telltale speech bubble only made her stomach churn more. What was wrong with her?

Fingers hovering over her phone's keyboard, Daisy waited, for what, she wasn't sure. Her trust had been violated again and again. But no singing angels would appear before her, bringing tidings of… anything. Though it was Eric's face that swam before her eyes, and Eric's texts that appeared in her mind's eye, it was her mother's voice that brought her the tidings she was waiting for, the permission she needed to learn to trust again.

Luke: We can walk on opposite sides of the street.

Daisy: And yell at each other the entire time? I don't think Mrs. Frothman would appreciate that.

Luke: We can call each other on the phone.

Daisy: Is that a ploy to get my number?

Luke: Did it work?

"Do it," she whispered, surprising herself with speaking the words aloud. She wanted this. She wanted to get to know Luke more, to explore the possibility of a relationship. And right now, he was giving every indication he might want the same. She sent Luke her number, and her heart beat a little faster, not yet knowing if this was another mistake, a mistake not as easily forgiven as paint on a canvas.

Luke: Thank you! We usually walk at 6 before I leave for work. I hope it's not too early for you.

Daisy: No, that's a great time. There won't be as many people out.

Any time before 10:00 AM was too early for Daisy, but in that moment, she was prepared to move the stars to spend time with Luke again.

Luke: So, is that a yes?

Daisy: Yes.

Luke: Great! I'll see you then!

Daisy looked up from her phone, noticing for the first time that the daisy in her mural was taller than the others. Its petals opened wide, and even with the simple Payne's Gray color, she'd captured the shading just right, as it faced the sun.

Pepper picked his way through the paint cans, somehow avoiding any colorful disasters. He sat on top of her feet, reaching up a gentle paw to touch her leg. Daisy picked him up, burying her face in his plush fur and accepting a tiny kiss on her cheek for her troubles.

For the second time that week, she was spending alone time with Luke Richards.

"Okay," Daisy whispered to the kitten, "maybe it is a date."

Buried in one of the boxes she'd brought was a stack of CD's. Daisy plucked one from the pile, and headed toward the living room, Pepper still tucked in the crook of her arm. Her mother's old music system sat beneath the television, dust-covered and well-loved. Daisy pressed the power button, and it buzzed to life. She inserted the disc and pressed play.

Music emanated from the speakers, and the kitten's ears perked up at the sound. Daisy turned the volume knob, and the bass thumped, vibrating through the floor. She spun in a circle, singing the first few lines to the kitten before heading back to her bedroom. She settled Pepper onto a pile of clothes and opened a can of Parchment White paint.

With an extra bounce in her movements, and the occasional solo session using a paintbrush as a makeshift microphone, both Daisy's spirit and the mural on her wall came to life. The sun and shadows moved across the walls and floor of the bedroom as the music played on, and the paint layered and popped against the once pink backdrop.

The passage of time was unbeknownst to Daisy. It wasn't until Mrs. Colton appeared in her doorway, arms folded with a bemused grin curling the corners of her mouth, did Daisy realize how late it was—and how off-key her duet with Freddie Mercury was.

"You've been busy," Mrs. Colton said.

Daisy lowered the paintbrush. "A little."

"Do you mind if I interrupt your concert in a bit? I'm having bingo with my friends."

Daisy's mouth fell open, her eyes widening. "What?"

"Over the internet, Daisy!"

"Oh," Daisy breathed, placing a paint-stained hand over her heart.

"I brought you something today, but it looks like you're plenty busy—"

"No, I… I could use a break."

Mrs. Colton reached into her purse, pulling out several squares of fabric. "A co-worker has been making masks, and she shared some of her fabric with me. I thought it might give you something to do. Besides consuming hours of pandemic news."

Daisy took the fabric diffidently. "I haven't turned the news on all day. But you're right. I might be over-reacting a bit." She flipped through the patterns, smiling when she saw the black cartoon cat.

"Well, I'd rather have you over-straining your voice than over-stressing. Would you like to join me tonight?"

Daisy flinched, biting her lip and clutching tighter to the fabric in her hand. "No, I… I—"

Mrs. Colton nodded. "You've always been shy around

strangers," she said, kissing Daisy's forehead. "If you change your mind, you know you'd be welcome."

"Thanks, but maybe I'll take you up on working on these masks. My hands could use a break."

"I think Freddie could too."

After another meal inspired by Chef Andrew, with a few creative liberties on Daisy's part, Mrs. Colton disappeared into the confines of her bedroom, leaving Daisy alone with Pepper and her thoughts.

Outside the bay window, Daisy watched the moths dance around the streetlamp in front of Mrs. Frothman's house. Her mother's laughing soon filtered down the hall. Perhaps she should have taken her up on the offer. The tiny voice in the back of her mind whispered more omens of judgement and betrayal, and Daisy pulled her knees to her chest. Not even Pepper's purring offered any comfort. Tomorrow morning couldn't come soon enough.

The headlights of Luke's sedan lit up the street before pulling into his drive. Even from inside, Daisy heard Apollo's excited barks. She watched him exit the vehicle, a bag of fast food beneath one arm. He raised a hand in greeting, and Daisy waved back. Again, she watched as he made his way inside, and through his living room blinds, saw Apollo dance excited circles around him.

Mrs. Colton belted a fierce guffaw. Pepper jumped from his seat before the window, trotting down the hall to investigate.

Don't go, Daisy thought. She didn't want to be alone. How could a day filled with music and happiness be replaced so quickly with the overwhelming dread of isolation?

Luke's ringtone went off in Daisy's pocket. She furrowed her brow, grabbing the phone and looking out the window again. Luke stood at his own front window, staring back, and waved.

Luke: Hey

Daisy: Hey

Luke: You okay?

She should have been okay. She was seeing Luke again tomorrow. The thought of it thrilled her. So why did she feel so awful?

Daisy: I don't know. It's complicated.

Luke: Like Arizona complicated?

Daisy stared across the street at Luke. He leaned over the back of his couch. Even from where she sat, she could see the tress of hair that casually fell across his face, his head tilted at her, waiting for a reply.

Arizona complicated. Daisy felt nothing but isolated in Arizona. And the moment she made a break for it, new circumstances forced her back into solitude. Isolation was all she knew. Isolation was safe. Isolation was…

Daisy: This is really lonely.

She watched Luke read her message, then turn his attention to Apollo. Daisy hung her head. Even Luke wanted nothing to do with her unless it was convenient for him. She uncurled her legs, preparing to stand when her phone rang again.

Luke: Go get a dry erase marker. And some glass cleaner.

Daisy turned, but Luke had disappeared from the couch.

Daisy: Okay. Why?

Luke: Meet me back at your window.

Confused, Daisy hurried to the kitchen, digging out an unopened pack of dry erase markers from the junk drawer, and glass cleaner from beneath the sink. She tucked a roll of paper towels beneath her arm and headed back to the bay window. To her surprise, Luke stood amongst her mother's tulips, waving and smiling just outside the parlor window. Daisy sat on the window seat, and though she was still utterly confused, she smiled again.

"What are you doing?" she mouthed at Luke.

He uncapped his own dry erase marker, drawing four crisscrossing lines on the window, and placed an O in the very center.

Daisy chuckled. Shaking her head, she uncapped her own marker and drew an X in the upper corner. He drew another O at the bottom of the column she was trying to fill in, so she placed an X at the end of the row. Luke blocked her move at the top of the center row, and she did the same at the bottom.

The games continued for several minutes. They expanded to a twelve-grid style, and the strategies became more difficult.

"Now you're just letting me win," Daisy said through the glass as she wiped the window clean on her side.

Luke drew a new board, turning his O into a heart. "Maybe I am."

Daisy looked away, not only for the flush that rose in her face but to push away the pit that had formed in her stomach. She turned back, her eyes looking deep into Luke's.

"Why are you doing this?"

Luke shrugged. "It was a rough day at work. I wanted to do something fun. Plus, I like you. You're smart and funny. And I think you're pretty. Double motivation."

Daisy giggled, the pit in her stomach turning to

butterflies and the blush growing stronger.

Mrs. Colton laughed again, and Daisy heard her mother bidding farewell to her friends.

"My mom's coming. I need to go." Daisy said. The last thing she wanted was for her mother to find her flirting with Luke through the window in the middle of the night. She was a grown adult, but it didn't mean she wanted to deal with the teasing.

Luke quickly wiped his side of the window. He glanced over Daisy's shoulder, and Daisy followed his gaze. Mrs. Colton was still in her room. She turned back and froze, her breath held tight. Luke stood so close to the window, if the pane had not been there to separate them, she would have felt his breath on her face. He held her gaze, their breath fogging the window between them.

"Parting is such sweet sorrow, that I shall say good night till it be morrow."

He winked and disappeared through the flowerbed, appearing in the light of the streetlamp when he reached the sidewalk. Daisy watched him dart across the street, slipping into his house and greeting Apollo again as if he'd been gone for days.

"What are you doing?"

Daisy jumped a mile. Her mother stood in the living room, one hand on her hip.

"Just... playing some tic-tac-toe," Daisy said. She raised the paper towel to the window, wiping away the vestiges of her game with Luke, and hiding the remnants of his breath on the exterior of the glass until it had faded.

Pepper bounded onto the window seat, his front paws pressed against the glass, staring outside.

"Maybe try paper next time," Mrs. Colton said, shaking her head. "Don't stay up too late, Sunshine. Good night."

"Right. Good idea. Uh, goodnight."

Luke's living room light went dark, and Pepper's ears swiveled in curiosity. Daisy let out a cleansing breath as her phone vibrated beneath her thigh.

Luke: Goodnight, Juliet.

day 14

The stars shone through a clear sky outside Daisy's window as Pepper purred beside her head. She tossed and turned, conflicting emotions rising and falling in her like the rising and falling of the kitten's gentle purr.

Was she *in love* with Luke? She'd given herself permission to accept his friendship. She'd given herself permission to explore the possibility of a relationship. There was no denying her fanciful crush had grown the last few weeks, but she couldn't shake the feeling it was simply the fact he was interacting with her during a tumultuous time that made her feel so strange around him.

"I think you're pretty." But he had seen her without makeup, in her most grimy of clothes and greasiest of hair. He had to be playing her. That was the answer.

Eric had sent one last voice message as Daisy climbed into bed. She'd done well ignoring them throughout the day, but the feeling Luke had risen in her, drove her to look at them.

"Stop ignoring me. What's wrong with you? You know you don't even deserve me, and I'm here putting in all this effort to help you. And you don't even have the courtesy to text me back."

Daisy wanted to text him back, to tell him all the wonderful things Luke had said and done for her in the last two weeks. To tell Eric how he'd failed her, and how Luke had picked up her broken pieces without even asking. But she couldn't burn that bridge. Not yet. If things didn't work out with Luke, she needed a safety net. If she was as dumb as Eric always said, if she couldn't do this on her own, she couldn't send that message. Not yet.

It felt like she'd barely shut her eyes when Daisy's alarm blared beside her. She searched through blurry eyes, slamming her finger on anything that felt remotely like her phone screen until the alarm quieted. Pepper stood, arching his back into a cartoonish Halloween cat stretch before laying back down on her pillow.

"Glad one of us got some sleep," Daisy mumbled, shoving off the covers and shuffling to the bathroom.

The hot water did little to energize her as she fumbled through a shower, using body wash on her hair instead of shampoo at first by mistake. At least she could go back to bed later.

Luke's ringtone sounded on the bathroom counter as Daisy reached for the bath towel. She dried her hands, grabbing for the phone as she still dripped into the tub.

Luke: I left something for you on the doorstep.

What on earth? Daisy thought. She finished toweling dry, hastily throwing on the clothes she'd laid out before bed. Mrs. Colton lay asleep as Daisy crept down the hall with Pepper, now finished sleeping, on her heels.

On the front step was a small gift bag. Daisy looked across the street at Luke's house, but it was eerily quiet in the twilight before dawn. She shooed her kitten back inside and extracted a small leash and harness from the bag. The harness looked new, but the faded star pattern and frays around the looped end indicated it had been well-used before this.

Daisy: What am I supposed to do with this?

Luke: Some kittens like to go for walks too. You can teach them how to walk on a leash and harness. I thought you might like to try it.

Daisy: You tell me this, minutes before I'm supposed to meet you for our walk?

Luke: You can try it next time if you prefer.

Daisy: You're implying there's a next time.

Luke: Not a morning person?

Daisy: Not in the slightest…

The kitten leapt onto Daisy's lap, sniffing and pawing at the items. They must have smelled like Luke and Apollo to him, Daisy thought. A scent he may have associated with the toys Luke had given him.

"I guess we're doing this," she said to the kitten.

The internet was full of videos depicting practically lifeless felines when wrangled into a harness. She put the tangle of straps over the kitten's head, and Pepper immediately nipped at the strap.

"Come on, Pepper. Work with me here," Daisy begged.

There was no way this would work. She found the feather wand Luke had gifted. A desperate ploy to distract the kitten as she fitted the rest of the harness to his body. It seemed to work. He took little notice of her adjustments thereafter. She checked the spacing with her fingers, ensuring it wasn't too tight or too loose. Pepper only pounced at her fingers, eager to play when the feather wand fell to the floor again. She shook her head. Just once Daisy would like to know something about herself and *her* cat before Luke did.

Daisy: Meet you outside?

Luke: On my way!

Daisy clipped the thin leash to Pepper's harness, and

the kitten obliged her tuttings, following her out the door. Luke stood on his own front step, Apollo sitting patiently at his side. He waved at Daisy, pointing to his phone before calling.

"Hey, you ready?" he asked.

"Hi, yeah, sure. Which way are we going?"

"I usually head toward High Street. I see Pepper's joining us."

Daisy cocked her head. "How did you know he'd do that?"

"I honestly didn't," Luke said, beginning his walk toward High Street. "But I figured it was worth a try. Oh, and thanks again for that picture of Apollo. I put it on the TV stand."

"It was nothing—"

"You keep saying that, but you're so good, Daisy. You're better than good. Have you considered teaching art classes online? It might give you a source of income until the quarantine's over."

Daisy stared at her feet as they walked. Pepper jogged ahead of her, keeping pace and only stopping to investigate the occasional strange smell. "I appreciate the compliment, but I'm not as good as you think. I'm just a waitress. That's about the only thing I'm good at."

"Well, I don't believe that. Not for one minute. And I'm sorry anyone ever made *you* believe it."

Daisy went silent, her fraught attempts failing to read between the lines of what Luke meant. What he really meant. She knew how to read Eric, or at least she thought she did. His snide remarks about her looks and her diets were his ways of showing he cared. That's what she told herself. That's what she made herself believe. It was the only way to survive. Until she finally let herself believe the truth.

"You okay over there? Did I say something wrong?" Luke's voice came over the phone, breaking Daisy from her sleep-deprived thoughts.

"No. I mean, yes. I mean… it's complicated."

"Like whether you enjoyed being in Arizona complicated?"

Daisy paused. It was the third time he'd used those words. If anything was going to come of her relationship with Luke, she wanted him to know sooner than later. He needed to know what he was getting into, that she was damaged goods. He could end it now, end it before she was too deeply hurt again.

"My ex has been texting me." Daisy looked at Luke as she spoke, afraid he'd reject her right there, afraid he'd stop in his tracks, red-faced, and remind her how awful it was that she'd been lying to him this whole time. But he just nodded his head, nodded like he knew all along.

"Are you okay with that?"

"It… it's—"

"Complicated."

"Yeah."

"Do you want him texting you, Daisy?"

The question hung between them, still and quiet

like the morning. It was a fair question, but what gave Daisy pause was not how Luke's tone was the opposite of what she'd expected. It was calm and understanding. What gave her pause the most was she didn't know the answer.

"I… I don't know," she mustered against some inner conflict she couldn't identify.

They stopped at the corner of High Street, and Daisy waited for Luke to cross the two sets of crosswalks before continuing.

"My parents divorced when I was really little. I actually don't even remember my dad very much. But my mom always made sure to tell me good stories about him and I. Most of my memories are the stories my mother told, and to me, my dad was like a superhero. When I got older, I asked her why they divorced if he was such a great guy. She told me she never said my father was a good man, but he was a good dad, and she wanted me to have those stories and memories. She said, you can love someone as a person and not love the things they do or say. Does that make sense?"

Daisy furrowed her brow. "Tha—that sounds…"

"Complicated, I know. I don't know how long this ex has been in your life, but—"

"He was my high school sweetheart," Daisy blurted out. Why had she said that? She pressed her palm to her face. Why did it even matter?

"That makes sense," Luke said.

"It does?" Daisy replied, removing her hand and

staring stunned across the street.

"Yeah, and it's okay if things are complicated. He's been a part of your life for a long time. He'll always be a part of your life. But you can choose how much a part. Does that make sense?"

"A bit, yes."

A text notification interrupted their conversation. Daisy pulled the phone from her ear, realizing she never informed her mother she was joining Luke and Apollo for their morning walk. She swiped at the text notification and stopped in her tracks. It was not her mother.

"You need to let this go. I know you think I'm controlling you, but everything I've done was to protect you. Daisy, you need to come home. You're not well. Let me get you some help."

"Hailing Lieutenant Colton. Communication frequencies open. You okay over there?"

Daisy quickly put the phone to her ear again, untangling herself from the leash Pepper had wound around her while she stood transfixed over her phone.

"Yes, I—I'm fine. It's fine."

She continued walking, her pace almost matching the pounding of her heart.

"You don't sound fine," Luke said tentatively. "Did the governor release a statement or something? Did something happen?"

He matched her pace, and Daisy could hear the jingle of Apollo's collar from across the street. Pepper, on the other hand, struggled to keep stride, his little legs stretched out, bounding to stay in step. Daisy stopped, and the kitten flopped over at her feet.

"You're right," Daisy said to Luke. "I don't like the things he says to me. It's why I left."

The chill March air seemed to cut right through her. She wrapped her free arm around her body, whether for physical or emotional comfort, she wasn't sure, but it wasn't the same. Eric had hurt her, and though he was halfway across the country, he was still hurting her. He may not have meant it. It was possible he didn't even know what he was doing, but it didn't change the fact that he had twisted her up into so many knots she was barely recognizable from the person she used to be. So tangled and twisted that the moment she allowed her heart to open to someone new, she didn't know how to react when Luke didn't respond the way she'd expected.

She needed someone to wrap their arms around her, to hold her tight and tell her, without words, that everything would be okay. But the one person who could do that safely due to the pandemic, she'd left blocks away, still sleeping in her childhood home. Daisy looked up at Luke, remembering his scent of bergamot and oakmoss, and felt a shiver run through her.

"Can I help?" Luke stood on the other side of the street, squarely facing her. Even from a distance, Daisy could see the lines of concern drawn on his face. Apollo must have felt his owner's mood. The dog sat at Luke's feet, calm and patient.

"I don't know," she said, her body still turned away. "I know that sounds stupid—"

"It's not stupid, Daisy. Anyone who's told you otherwise is a fool. You're not stupid."

"Yes, I am! You don't have to patronize me! I know when I'm being irrational!" Her voice echoed in the gray light of morning as she dropped her free arm, clenching her fist in rage. She heard Luke take a deep breath. She closed her eyes tight and clenched her teeth, waiting for the blow of rejection to finally fall. She just wanted this over with.

"I'm sorry I upset you, but I promise you aren't being stupid or irrational. And I won't let you say those things about yourself either."

Daisy opened her eyes. Through the hot, salty tears that stung her vision, she could see Luke still standing on the other side of the street. He was relaxed, one hand holding the phone, the other gently scratching Apollo's ear.

"How can you say that? You don't even know me."

"Because you're not. And because I like you."

Daisy's breath hitched as his words struck her heart. Why did it hurt? Why were the bad things so much easier to believe? This was not the reaction she had prepared herself for.

"You're right. I don't know you. Not very well. But I want to. I want to know everything there is to know about you, Daisy Colton."

"Why?" The words came barely as a whisper, so quiet she wasn't sure she'd even spoken them.

"Because you're my friend. Because I care about you. Because you're my Juliet, and I don't want to see you hurt."

Pepper pawed at Daisy's leg, giving a wide, toothy meow. It was his way of asking to be held. Daisy obliged, wiping the tears from her face before the kitten covered her in sandpaper kisses.

"I don't have any friends," Daisy replied, the strength returning to her voice.

"You do now."

Apollo yipped, and Luke turned back toward their neighborhood. Daisy followed, still holding the kitten in her arms as they walked in silence, listening to the world awaken around them.

"Have you ever read Ray Bradbury?" Luke asked as they re-crossed High Street.

Daisy blinked away the last of her tears. "A few."

"I think he said it best. *We cannot tell the precise moment when friendship is formed. As in filling a vessel drop by drop, there is at last a drop which makes it run over; so in a series of kindnesses there is at least one which makes the heart run over.*"

Daisy sniffed. "I don't think I remember that one."

"Fahrenheit 451."

"I could never bring myself to read a book about burning books."

Luke chuckled. "I don't blame you."

Daisy didn't speak. She didn't have to. Luke filled the silence as they walked. It felt good to listen to his voice, not having to think or feel or do. She listened as he talked about watching *The Halloween Tree* as a child, and how it was the first book by Ray Bradbury he read. She listened, and she breathed, and soon she stood at the end of the driveway to her childhood home, with its overflowing gardens and her little white car.

"I'll help you, Daisy. I'll help you in whatever way I can, and however you want me to. And not because I don't think you can do it by yourself. Because that's what friends do."

Daisy set Pepper at her feet, an idea forming in her mind. "You wouldn't happen to know where I can get a new cellphone, do you?"

Even from across the street, Daisy saw the smile spread over Luke's face. "I do, actually. A friend of mine works at Cell-o-rama. I'll text you his number."

"That... that would be great."

She hadn't expected Luke to have an answer. She thought she'd have to do it all herself. Because that's what freedom was, wasn't it? A light came on somewhere in her home, and Daisy checked the time on her phone. She didn't yet know how she would pay for a new cellphone, but she never wanted to yell at Luke like that again. If that meant taking proper action to cut Eric from her life, it was a risk she was willing to... at least consider.

"I have to go to work," Luke said, the disappointment

in his voice clear. "Are you going to be okay?"

"I'm fine. Mom has today off."

Luke nodded. "You have my number now, so reach out if you need me. I'll talk to you later, Daisy."

Daisy watched Luke and Apollo turn and leave. She stared at the empty front porch step, knowing she didn't deserve his friendship. She'd done nothing to earn it, and she didn't know if she was strong enough to keep it. As the sun rose above the horizon, Daisy closed her own front door behind her and unclipped Pepper from his harness. She collapsed onto the heather-gray sofa, pulling her father's afghan around her. Moments later, she heard her mother's footsteps padding down the hall and into the living room.

"Daisy, where did you go?" The concern in Mrs. Colton's tone was unmistakable.

"For a walk with Luke and Apollo," Daisy replied. "I'm sorry, I forgot to tell you. It won't happen again."

Mrs. Colton joined Daisy on the couch, inviting Pepper onto her lap with a little pat. "Eric still messaging you?"

Daisy handed over her phone in answer. Mrs. Colton scrolled through the ignored messages, her jaw clenched.

"How did you do it, Mom?" Daisy finally asked. "How did you let go after Papa died? How did you know you'd be okay, that you could do everything on your own?"

Mrs. Colton let out a lengthy sigh. "I didn't know,

Sunshine. I really didn't. And you know what? Sometimes I failed. I almost lost my car."

"What?" Daisy spun around, her eyes wide.

"Yeah. It slipped through the cracks. A pretty big thing to slip, but it did. Patty had to give me a loan until I received some of Papa's life insurance to pay her back."

"I didn't know that." Guilt swept through Daisy, and she pulled the afghan tighter around her.

"It wasn't anything you needed to worry about, Sunshine. And I paid Patty back the money. Or at least what she allowed me to pay back. That's what friends do, my love. You don't have to do this alone."

Mrs. Colton placed the cellphone in her daughter's hand. Daisy glanced through Eric's messages again as a message from Luke flashed across the top of the screen.

Luke: I talked to Casey. He's my friend at Cell-o-rama. He said he's happy to help and you can call him anytime. Thanks for the walk this morning. Spending time with you helps get me through my day a little easier.

"I don't want to," Daisy said, more to herself than her mother. "I don't want to do this alone anymore. I won't."

day 17

The roads were oddly void of traffic. The occasional truck with DIY lettering for a small business or zippy little electric car dotted the streets of the main city a few miles outside of Erie River, but gone was the typical bumper to bumper traffic. A bright blue sky shone overhead, and Daisy recalled news reports of decreased air pollution causing an uptick in environmental healing. She pulled into the parking lot of Cell-o-rama and wondered if today's blue sky was because of less traffic, or simply a result of the unpredictable weather for Ohio in March.

Empty parking spaces spanned on either side of Daisy's car. A fast-food restaurant sat on the other side of the lot with seagulls circling what was typically an over-flowing dumpster. Instead, they pecked and scavenged the meager findings scattered around the building. "Rats with Wings," Mrs. Colton would have called them. It wasn't unusual to see gulls so far inland.

Not when the city was rife with dumpsters full of free food. But Daisy hadn't seen a seagull since she'd left for Arizona. Somehow, the gray and white scavengers seemed like an omen as she pulled her phone from her purse.

Eric: I'm really worried about you, Daisy. I know you're staying with your mom. Remember, I put that tracker on your phone a few years ago? I did it to protect you, so if you ran off like this, I could find you and help you. Listen, if I don't hear back from you, I'm coming up to Erie River to get you.

Eric's relentless tries to get a hold of Daisy lasted throughout the night. He'd most likely burned through all his side girlfriends and was now both bored and sexually desperate. His minutes' long voice mails in the middle of the night eventually forced Daisy to turn her phone off all together.

He begged her to come back. He said he was lost without her, seeing his past faults and vowing to change. But Daisy saw now his words of concern, his pleas of despair were nothing more than veiled threats to regain the control she'd taken from him.

Her fingers hovered over the draft message she and Mrs. Colton sat up late into the night discussing. Breaking up over text was not Daisy's style. She cringed each time she saw it in the movies, or when Mel dumped whatever boy-toy she was dating that month. But it seemed the safer option. If Daisy heard the pleading in Eric's voice during a live call, if he said just the right thing, she worried she'd fall for his lies again. She had to do this now.

Daisy: Eric, I'm not coming back. You will always have a place in my heart, but I've come to realize this is not the life I want. It's not fair to either of us to keep living this lie. Do not follow me and do not contact me. Goodbye.

Daisy closed her eyes and pressed Send. She sat there for several long minutes, eyes shut tight, and her face growing hot from her steady breathing beneath her mask. No reply came. The phone didn't vibrate or ring in her hand with Eric's frantic attempts to woo her back. No chimes signaling a new message sat waiting in her inbox. Silence. Just silence. It was over.

A weight seemed lifted from her chest, and Daisy couldn't help but think of Frodo at the end of *Return of the King*. She didn't realize the hold Eric had on her until it was no longer there. She vowed then and there that no one would hold that kind of power over her again.

Daisy tied and adjusted the mask on her face, one she had made from the black cat fabric her mother gifted her. She'd left a dog-themed one in Luke's mailbox before leaving that afternoon, and the thought made her smile. Pursuing a relationship with Luke Richards seemed less of a fanciful fairy tale, now that she was free.

She pulled a disinfectant wipe from the container—she was running low—and wiped down her current phone. Reaching for the bag of gloves her mother had nicked from work, Daisy hesitated. Luke's words about PPE being more difficult to obtain ran through her mind. As did the reports that gloves didn't help most people anyway since they weren't used properly. Instead, she popped the tiny bottle of hand sanitizer she kept in the car into her purse and headed into the store.

We ask that all our patrons consider wearing a mask for the safety of our team members, customers, and you. Hope your day is Cell-o-tastic!

Daisy smiled at the sign on the door as she entered. Again, the silence of the store hung in the air like a strange soundtrack to the pandemic times. A skinny redhead man looked up from behind the counter, and Daisy watched his eyes crinkle with a smile when he saw her.

"You must be Daisy," the man said, making his way onto the main floor. "I'm Casey. It's a pleasure to meet you. I hope you don't mind, we're not shaking hands at the moment."

"I don't mind at all," Daisy said, returning her bottle of hand sanitizer into her purse after touching the door.

Casey tucked his thumbs behind a pair of decorative red suspenders and leaned back on his heels. "What can I help you with today? Luke didn't give me any specifics."

"I need a new phone," Daisy muttered. Of course, she needed a new phone. Why else would she be here? She refrained from burying her face in her hands out of embarrassment. At least she hadn't said *I need a new phone to better run away from my past*. Though true, it didn't exactly seem like the appropriate thing to say, especially to one of Luke's friends.

"Well, you've come to the right place," Casey assured her without skipping a beat. "Any particular model you've been looking at? Who's your cell carrier?"

"I…" *You can do this. He's Luke's friend. Trust him.* "I don't know. I've never done this before. This is kind of my first phone. I mean, I've had phones before, but… I'll be paying for it."

"Well, congratulations. Or should I say, con-*cat*-ulations?" Casey smiled again, pointing at the cartoon cats on Daisy's mask. "He's already used that one on you, hasn't he?" Casey's eyes filled with disappointment.

"Unfortunately," Daisy mused. Yes, there was no doubt Casey was Luke's friend, and she smiled at the thought of the two getting into all kinds of mischief.

"Typical. He's always stealing my best lines," Casey said, shaking his head. "Come on. I've got a little questionnaire to help us. We'll go through how you want to use the phone, any special applications you have or need, your budget. Then we can start playing with some floor models."

He led her back to the counter, pulling out a spray

bottle of disinfectant. From behind a wall of clear plexiglass, Casey wiped down both sides of the counter and Daisy's stool before handing the bottle off to his co-worker with a nod. He placed a pen and paper on the counter before him with a little flourish and clicked his pen a few times before gesturing for Daisy to sit.

Daisy sat on the offered stool, casting a glance to the customer beside her. She leapt out of her seat, clutching at her purse strap and taking several steps back.

"Miss? Are... are you okay?" the second Cell-o-rama employee asked as the customer turned to face her.

Daisy blinked at the man sitting on the stool across from her. He had the same muscular build, the same military-style haircut. Even his nose was similar. But this was not Eric.

"I'm... I'm sorry. I thought you were... someone I knew." Daisy sat back on the stool again, facing a concerned Casey through the plexiglass wall.

She took several calming breaths, her hands still shaking. If there were ever a sign she was ready to let go of the past, that she *needed* to break free, this was it. She was over being a victim. She was ready to be a survivor, and whatever lay beyond that.

Casey clipped the pen to his suspender and folded the piece of paper into his pocket.

"Follow me," he said with a wink.

Daisy held tight to her purse strap like it was some protective armor across her chest. She followed Casey, quite confused, behind the counter, and through a side door. A large folding table with a handful of folding chairs sat in the middle of the employee break room. It was decorated with a Happy Birthday banner, the R looking a little worse for wear as it barely clung to the string.

Casey propped open a back door that led to the parking lot and quickly wiped the table with disinfectant.

"Communal areas are off-limits, but being the assistant manager has its perks," Casey said. He opened the fridge, pulling out a water bottle and handing it to Daisy.

"Thanks," Daisy said, tentatively.

"My cousin's first husband was a right twat-waffle," Casey said, pulling the paper from his pocket and taking a seat at the far end of the table. "She was hyperaware for months after the divorce. Anyway, we can get started on the questionnaire when you're ready."

An hour later, Daisy held a refurbished version of last year's model smartphone, complete with a case and other accessories Casey pulled from the shelf saying they were "already taken care of."

"After I finish importing your contacts, we can send a message to everyone with your new phone number," Casey informed her from behind the sheet of clear plexiglass once more.

"No!" Daisy cried, blushing. "Sorry, I—I'll do it myself. There are... certain people I don't want to have my new number."

Casey nodded, his eyes flicking up to the now empty seat of the customer who had startled Daisy. "Fair enough. It happens more often than you think."

"Thanks," Daisy said, trying to break her habit of touching her face in a nervous fidget.

"So, how long have you and Luke been seeing each other?"

Daisy froze, her hand poised above the contract she was in the middle of signing. "Not... not very long. I've only been back a couple of weeks."

"The way he talks about you, I'd have thought it was a while."

"He... he talks about me?" Daisy pushed the paper back beneath the plexiglass, eyes sparkling with excitement.

Casey laughed. "You're all he talks about lately. I guess that timeline makes sense now that you mention it. He's completely smitten. There. You're all set." He handed her the new phone, and though his face was half-obscured by his mask, there was no denying the smug smile on his face.

"Thanks, Casey."

"Any time, Daisy. I hope to see you around when this is all over."

"Me too," she said, her tone genuine. "Maybe I'll be able to shake your hand next time."

She left Cell-o-rama, her bag loaded down with pre-sanitized accessories, and a similar smug smile to

Casey's. She pulled the mask from her face, wiping the sweat from her upper lip, and texted Luke.

Daisy: This is Daisy. New phone number.

Luke: Great! Did Casey behave himself?

Daisy: Yes, Casey was great. In fact, he was quite chatty.

Luke: Oh, no… what did he say?

Daisy: Nothing much. But he had a bunch of phone accessories he said were already paid for. You wouldn't happen to know anything about that, would you Batman Butt?

Luke: Guilty. I hope I didn't overstep anything.

Daisy: At least let me make it up to you.

Luke: Dinner tonight?

Daisy paused. The thought of going to the grocery store again wasn't the most pleasant. But if Luke really wanted her to make him something…

Daisy: I suppose I could run to the store. What are you in the mood for?

Luke: I mean, will you have a virtual dinner with me again tonight? To make up for the wireless charger and case and stuff, like you said. I promise to wear pants.

Daisy smiled at the retort that came to her mind, but restrained herself from sending it.

Daisy: I guess if you promise, then you have a deal.

Setting her new phone in the passenger seat, Daisy put her car in drive. The tensions she'd experienced from the misidentified stranger were gone, replaced with the excited anticipation of dinner, again, with Luke Richards.

"Your date food is here!" Mrs. Colton called down the hall, bumping the front door closed with her hip.

Daisy burst out of the bathroom, bath towel wrapped around her body, and her hair freshly blow-dried.

"Or is it still not a date?" Mrs. Colton teased.

Daisy checked the tuck of her towel, then proceeded into the kitchen to wipe down the contents of the bag. "Does this makeup look like not a date to you?"

"I think you're beautiful even without makeup." Mrs. Colton kissed her daughter's cheek, stealing a tortilla chip Daisy had just dumped into a bowl.

"Hey!"

"It's a match-making fee!" she said and stole one last chip before disappearing into the living room.

With Pepper hot on her heels, Daisy juggled the various containers of food into her bedroom and shut the door. She distracted the kitten with a tin of food as she shuffled through her suitcases. She didn't have many clothes, and even if she had the money to buy more, all the stores were currently closed. With a huff, she abandoned the suitcases and threw open her closet as Luke's text message came through.

Luke: Ready, Freddie?

Daisy: Be there in a minute!

Luke: No problem. Send the video request when you're ready.

Daisy tossed the phone on her bed, turning back to her closet. It was like a time capsule back to the mid-2000s, complete with prom dresses and hip-hugger jeans she'd probably be lucky to squeeze one thigh into.

At the back of her closet was a stretchy red dress she'd worn for her school's Christmas formal. That was the year Homecoming had been cancelled. The entire football team - and a few cheerleaders and band girls - ended up with mono. She hoped it was still stretchy enough.

Daisy pulled the dress from the hanger and wiggled into it. She looked at herself in the mirror as Pepper started his after-meal bath. Either her chest had gotten significantly bigger since high school, or Mrs. Colton made some rather questionable decisions in what she allowed her daughter to wear in high school. Daisy threw on a lacey cropped shawl, opened her laptop, and sent the video request to Luke.

"Wow. You look beautiful," he said as soon as she came on screen. "That was totally worth the wait."

Daisy blushed. "I didn't bring a lot of clothes with me. This was in my closet from high school. I'm surprised it still fits."

"Well, now I feel underdressed. Do you want me to go change?"

"No," Daisy said, her voice an octave or two higher than she intended. "No, I just thought you might be tired of seeing me in that old sweater is all."

"Daisy Colton, you could wear nothing, and I'd never get tired of seeing you."

Daisy giggled as Luke's hands covered his face.

"I cannot believe I said that. I am so sorry."

Daisy laughed and shooed Pepper away from the tacos on her plate.

"I'll forgive you. Besides, that shade looks great on you."

Luke blushed even more.

"I didn't ask. I hope you like Mexican. Macho Taco is one of my favorite places."

"I love Mexican."

"Oh, good," Luke said, tucking into his meal. "So, Casey got you all set up then?"

Daisy nodded through a mouthful of taco and swallowed before replying. "Yes. He was a perfect gentleman. You could learn a thing or two."

"Are you saying I'm not a gentleman?" Luke

pointed an exaggerated hand toward himself, taco grease staining the corners of his lips.

"All I said was you might learn a thing or two. Take it as you will."

"Well, I think I'll take that as a challenge, my lady. Hey, did you paint your wall?"

Daisy looked at the mural behind her. "Oh, yeah. I forgot."

"Can I see it?"

Daisy shrugged, lifting the laptop into the air, and panning from one side to the other.

"Wow. That's amazing. And you did that in one day?" Luke asked.

"It's not quite finished yet, but yeah."

"That's incredible."

Daisy returned the laptop to its perch upon the stack of books on her end table and shrugged, popping a chip in her mouth.

"Eric would say it looks childish."

Daisy had subconsciously reached for her phone throughout the day, even though she hadn't given Eric her new number. While her newfound freedom was liberating, she felt strangely disconnected. His words of coming to Erie River still haunted her, though she knew his threats were almost always empty. Almost. It was strange not to get them, to know she'd never get them again. Because, at least for once, he had been paying attention to her.

"Well, Eric's wrong. You'll have to forgive me if I

don't think highly of someone who hurt my friend." Luke chugged the remainder of his wine, shaking out his arms as if psyching himself up.

"Okay, I've thought of a game. Or a topic, whatever you want to call it," he said.

Daisy raised an eyebrow. "Have you now?"

Luke cleared his throat. "If you could have three wishes, what would they be?"

"What?" Daisy sat up, abandoning the rest of her tacos. "That is a very specific question."

Luke, on the other hand, raised his plate to his chin, and shoved half a taco in his mouth before replying, "You can learn a lot about a person from that question."

"Hmm…" Daisy swirled her own wine in her glass. "I can wish for anything?"

"You can't wish for more wishes," Luke said with a wink.

"Of course not! Robin Williams would have my head!"

"See, you go with *Aladdin*, and I'm over here thinking *Shazam*."

Daisy threw her head back and laughed. She heard Luke laugh through the computer speakers, which only made her giggle more.

"I love your laugh," she heard him say. It was easy to laugh around Luke, and she laughed more with him in the last two weeks than she had in years with Eric.

Daisy took a long drink of her wine, trying to pretend she hadn't heard the compliment.

"Three wishes," she mused. "Well, I guess the first would be financial stability. I wouldn't want to wish for a specific amount of money, but rather have a blanket of financial stability. I think it would give me the freedom to do things. Like take Mom on that trip to Scotland, buy a house, things like that. No matter what decision I made, I'd always be stable, you know? Is that a loophole?"

Luke nodded. "Even if it weren't, it's very practical of you. Wish number two."

"Um..." Daisy chewed the corner of a tortilla chip. "I think I'd like to go to culinary school."

Luke set his plate on the floor where Daisy assumed Apollo was acting as a pre-wash cycle.

"Culinary school? Wow."

She shrugged. "I mean, I already have an arts degree, and that didn't exactly pan out how I planned. I was thinking I could be a restaurant consultant."

"Restaurant consultant?" Luke raised his eyebrows, seeming impressed.

"Yeah. I could use my art degree to design the restaurants, the plating presentation, the menus."

A smile slowly spread over Luke's face, freshly wiped clean of taco grease.

"What? Is that too silly of an idea? Do... do I have something on my face?"

"No, I think it's a fabulous idea. And that's the first time you've thought about something just for you since I met you."

Daisy wiped her face with a paper towel for good measure anyway, thankful for the no-budge lipstick she'd invested in. "Is… is that a bad thing?"

"Absolutely not. It was nice to hear you say something good about yourself. Because you have amazing art talent, Daisy. You really do. I know you'd excel in culinary school too."

She shrugged again, as if pretending her words were unimportant would make it so. "I guess it's just easier to believe the bad things people say. When someone puts you down long enough, you tend to start believing them."

"I'm sorry he hurt you," Luke said, his voice gentle. "I hope you know everything negative he ever said about you isn't true. You're talented and courageous, and he's a fool for not seeing it. It's his loss, and someday someone very lucky will fall madly in love with you."

Daisy turned away, tears stinging her eyes as she fought to keep them away. She took a deep breath, taking an enormous bite of her taco.

"This one's… a bit spicy," she lied.

Luke didn't question it. He didn't call her a crybaby or tell her to not be so stupid next time. He stared at her with such conviction, his eyes penetrating her soul as if he were trying to reach the broken part inside of her and mend it with just his gaze.

Daisy swallowed. "What about you? What would your three wishes be?"

Luke paused and turned away as if his mind were somewhere else completely. "I'd wish for world peace."

"World peace?"

"Not just between humans, but all animals. All life."

"So, you'd have us all be passive vegans? Is that your way of slowly taking over the world?"

Luke chuckled, whatever tension lay between them, now dissipating. "No. There's no world domination in my future. I mean actual, real peace. People shouldn't have to run away to destress, you know? Finding balance and harmony between nature and progress. Peace."

"Now you're making financial stability look amateur," Daisy said, wiping her hands clean and giving her own empty plate to Pepper.

"No, I just have wild dreams."

Luke looked at her through the screen again, his eyes connecting to hers, and for a moment, Daisy wondered if his wild dreams had anything to do with her. Because in her own wild dreams, Luke played a frequent starring role.

"What else?" she asked.

"That there would always be the perfect amount of pineapple on every pizza."

"Now you're just teasing me." She laughed.

"Daisy Colton, look at my face," Luke drew closer to the camera lens until his face took up the entire screen. "I have never been more serious in all my life. Especially about pineapple on pizza." He winked at her.

"Okay, fair enough. I know how you like your fruit monstrosities. So, what's your last wish?"

"Uh-uh, not till you say yours. I asked first."

Daisy invited Pepper onto her lap, giving her a moment to collect her thoughts. She scratched under the kitten's chin, tilting her head before answering.

"I think it's silly that you'd have to use all your wishes right away. The person I am now is not who I'll be in ten or fifty years. What if one of my grandchildren gets cancer? If I were to, say, wish for a boat now, that would be a terrible way to waste my wish. No, I think I'd hold on to my last wish."

Luke stared at the computer screen until his hazel eyes flicked up to the camera, looking directly at Daisy again.

"I wish I could kiss you right now," he said at last, taking her by surprise.

Daisy blushed, breaking eye contact. "I… I guess I wouldn't hate that wish."

"*And he took her in his arms and kissed her under the sunlit sky,*" Luke said, and when Daisy looked back at the screen, he still looked straight through her.

"*He cared not that they stood high upon the walls in the sight of many.* From *Return of the King,*" Daisy said. She was beyond blushing. Her stomach was in knots, and the hairs on her entire body stood on end. If there wasn't a computer separating them, Daisy wasn't sure what she'd have done. "Except I'm no Eowyn. I'm not even a real platinum blonde. Look." She tilted her head down, revealing the ash-blonde roots of her hair like she were giving away a terrible secret.

"No, you're my Juliet," Luke said so sincerely, Daisy's hands trembled.

Daisy shook her head. "I'm no noble lady or anything like that. I'm awkward and shy." What was she even saying? Why was she pushing him away? "I'm just... just a girl." It was a terrifying thought she didn't know how to process. That someone could want her as much as she wanted them.

"Well, if you're a girl standing in front of a boy asking him to love her, then I would definitely give my last wish for that."

Daisy took a deep breath. Even without him physically standing in front of her, she felt the passion between them. In that moment, Daisy realized Luke Richards was the one thing in the entire world she wanted more than anything, and the one thing the world was keeping from her.

"I thought we were just friends," she whispered.

"We are friends."

With her breath coming in shallow pulses, Daisy looked into the camera lens and lifted her hand to the computer screen. A smile tugged at the corner of Luke's mouth, placing his own hand on the computer screen. Daisy was weightless and heavy all at once. She was numb, and yet it felt like fire surged through her. This was the closest they could get to holding hands, and yet she wanted so much more.

She bit her lip, words completely failing her.

"Daisy—"

Apollo shoved his head under Luke's arm, pulling his hand away from the screen. Daisy let out a breath, sensation returning to her body as if she were freed from a curse.

"You have the worst timing," Luke said to the dog, scratching behind both his ears.

"Does he need taken out already?" Daisy asked, her heart rate returning to normal.

"No, he was just saying hi to you," Luke said. "I told you, Apollo likes you."

"Well, maybe Apollo should come over for another playdate, and I'll play with him this time."

"Apollo says that's a woof-er-ful idea," Luke said in his cartoonish Apollo voice, and Daisy laughed.

day 34

Daisy cracked their last egg into the skillet, watching the translucent whites turn a milky opaque. Pepper pawed at her leg. He'd grown considerably in the span of a few weeks. He was now long and lanky and still just as demanding.

"No, you had a piece of bacon," Daisy chided. "You don't need eggs too. Besides, this is mine."

Pepper tried pawing her foot one last time, then sauntered into the living room with a definite huff to his swagger.

Daisy shook her head as she dished up her breakfast. She sat at the kitchen table, shoving over the small pile of mail and other odds and ends her mother had tried to stack there. She pulled a college program guide from the pile, flipping to the culinary arts section. She'd narrowed down her choices to three schools, though she doubted her chances of getting into any of the New York schools.

She looked up from the catalog, a bite of egg perched at the end of her fork before her lips. Luke would not have approved of that attitude. She smiled at the thought of him scolding her from across the street, wagging his finger with one hand on his hip, which only made her smile more. Daisy reached for the butter dish, spreading the last of it on her English muffin. That would have to go on the list too.

Mrs. Colton was scheduled a late shift that night, and Luke was working a double. Daisy added *Butter* to the grocery list below *Eggs, Cat/Dog treats*, and *Flour Tortillas*. She set aside the catalog—she'd looked at it a dozen times before—and pulled out her phone, texting Luke.

Daisy: Heading to the store soon. Need anything?

Luke: Are you making your tacos tonight?

Daisy: Yes. And flour tortillas are already on the list.

Luke replied with several celebratory emojis. He loved her tacos. He claimed they were better than Macho Taco, but she still wasn't convinced. He usually inhaled them too quickly to appreciate the subtle nuance of flavor. Daisy had told him as much, but he'd only mumbled some kind of indiscernible defense with guacamole trailing from the corner of his mouth.

Daisy finished the last of her egg and set the plate on the floor, a habit Pepper wasn't about to let her break. He bounded into the kitchen and began polishing the plate.

Daisy went through the kitchen and bathroom one last time, checking off the items on her list. A surprising April snow fell outside, and her Arizona wardrobe was ill-equipped for such an event. She grabbed one of her mother's jackets from the closet before heading out. Brushing a thin layer of snow from her windshield, she climbed in, shivering like a Sphynx kitten in December. Winter was one thing she did *not* miss about Ohio, but who could have expected snow in April?

Apparently, it was a question everyone was asking— or all the panic-buyers had run out of their stockpiles of Twinkies and toilet paper. Daisy pulled into the grocery store parking lot, shocked at the number of vehicles. She hadn't seen this many people out since the first days of the quarantine. But snow generally had that effect on people in Ohio.

There was a line for the shopping carts as customers flooded into the store. Daisy waited on the little painter's tape X, six feet behind the shopper in front of her. The store's greeter pulled each cart from the row, spraying it with disinfectant and giving it a quick wipe down before handing it off.

"Here you are, dear. Oh, I love your mask!" the woman said, handing Daisy a damp cart.

Daisy pulled a disinfectant wipe from her purse, wiping down the cart again for good measure. "Thanks!" she said with a wave and hurried out of line.

She made her way to the back of the store first, grabbing eggs, butter, and the special iced coffee Luke liked to mix with his protein shakes in the morning. She rounded the corner, almost colliding with a customer ignoring the one-way stickers on the floor of the aisles.

"Watch where you're going, sheep," the man grumbled, shooting a nasty look at Daisy.

Daisy pulled her cart back, allowing the man through. He wasn't wearing a mask, and Daisy turned her head as he walked by. Masks only worked so well, if at all. She didn't want to breathe too deeply. A little shaken, she continued on, adding a box of pasta and a jar of sweet pickles to her cart.

The home essentials aisle was packed with shoppers going in all directions. The toilet paper was almost wiped out entirely, and despite the 2-item limit for disinfectant wipes, Daisy watched one woman load her cart down with at least twelve containers, smashing the six loaves of bread that lay at the bottom. Daisy quickly grabbed two containers, tucking them beneath her purse in the front seat. News reports abounded with shoppers stealing supplies from others' carts.

Checking off the items on her list, Daisy wove her way through the aisles as quickly as she could. She reached for a bag of apples and her blood ran suddenly cold. On the other side of the produce display stood a man with a familiar military-style haircut and red football jersey. He stared at his phone with a package of cookies tucked under one arm.

As he turned, Daisy took a step back. The man nodded an acknowledgment to her as he grabbed a bag of lemons and left. It wasn't Eric. She exhaled, though it was several moments before her body would move again.

Daisy snatched the bag of apples and ran for the checkout, abandoning the rest of the items that remained on her list. The snow fell in little clumps of light, dry flakes as she loaded her grocery bags into her car and climbed into the driver's seat. She ripped the mask off her face, pulling her phone from her purse.

She never gave Eric her new number after sending him her final message. She deactivated all her social media accounts, email addresses, and started fresh. Though she had added some friends and family from her previous account, she thought she'd been careful. The stranger in the store wasn't Eric, but the fear that gripped her, that still made her hands shake even now, made her question if she'd been too lax.

The snow built on her windshield as she scrolled through her accounts. There were no signs of Eric or any of his friends she'd been sure to block as well. She double-checked her privacy settings and forced herself to take several deep breaths.

It was just in her head, she told herself. Luke and Mrs.

Colton assured her that her fears and apprehensions were valid. She'd been traumatized for years, even if it wasn't in the typical way people thought of surviving such a relationship. She was allowed to be afraid, but she wouldn't let it control her.

"You're safe," she said aloud. "That was your past. He has no power over you anymore."

Through dangers untold and hardships unnumbered… Sarah Williams' quote from *The Labyrinth* had become like a mantra to Daisy, giving her a kind of strength that only the words of books and movies she used to escape to could do for her.

The thought of Luke offering to dress as the Goblin King for Halloween ran through her mind, and she smiled, easing some of her fears. She hung her mask from the review mirror and put her car in drive, heading for the safety of home.

Pepper followed Daisy in and out of the house, pouncing at the falling snowflakes as she unloaded her car into the kitchen. She only allowed him outside when he was with her. The kitten had caught on quickly, taking advantage of any time she allowed him outside. He never went further than the yard, but Daisy didn't trust him without a watchful eye. Pepper had proven himself to be too smart for his own good.

"Come on, Pepper. Get your furry tail inside," Daisy called to him.

Pepper took his time, making a show of swatting at a last few snowflakes before casually stepping through the front door. Daisy looked up and down the street, not exactly sure what she expected to see, and shut the front door.

Pepper settled on Daisy's lap as she fell onto the heather-gray sofa. She scrolled through her social media, seeing the same pictures over and over again from the few friends she had. Pepper stepped onto her chest, pushing his face into her chin. She kissed him, holding the phone up for yet another picture of her and the little black cat.

"Should we send Luke a picture to make him smile? Hmm?" she cooed at the little cat.

She snapped a few more pictures, ignoring the messaging alert that popped up at the top of her phone screen from someone named Larry she didn't even know. Daisy pulled up Luke's messages and sent three pictures of her and Pepper, each showing the kitten in states of progressively more annoyance.

Daisy: Pepper is not amused. Hope you're having a great day!

The message notification from Larry popped up again. Daisy swiped it away, settling onto the sofa with her little black kitten, her father's afghan, and another episode of Shelley Duvall. She drifted in and out of sleep as the snowflakes fell outside, and *The Tale of the Frog Prince* played on the television. When her message notifications pinged a third and final time, she opened her eyes and grabbed her phone.

Larry: I can't believe you've been cheating on me this whole time.

Larry: I'm giving you one last chance to come home. You better message me back.

Larry: I'm staying with friends in Erie River. I can forgive you, and we can pretend none of this ever happened. But if you don't reply back, I'll make sure Luke Richards never wants anything to do with you ever again.

He had found her. Daisy didn't know how, but Eric had found her. She pushed off the afghan, ignoring Pepper as he tumbled to the floor, and paced back and forth in front of the television, staring at the messages.

Larry the Cable Guy was Eric's favorite comedian. He must have chosen the fake identity to get around her social media block to spy on her. She read his words over and over again, trying to decipher their meaning.

I'll make sure Luke Richards never wants anything to do with you ever again.

"Luke." His name fell from her lips seconds before she bolted out the door.

Daisy jumped into her car and tore out of the driveway. After nearly ten years with Eric, she knew he was possessive, and above all else, impulsive. He must have tired of his one or two night flings with the girls Daisy knew all too well he chatted up and flirted with online. He may have even been drunk when he decided to chase Daisy halfway across the country. If he *was* in Erie River. Was that a chance she was willing to take?

And if he was acting impulsively, acting on the idea that Daisy was still his...

Daisy rolled through several stop signs, trying to make her way to the Erie River EMS and Fire Station as the snow continued to fall around her little car. Its tires were designed for desert conditions, unfit for the cold and unpredictable weather of Ohio, and they easily slid across the asphalt in the slushy road conditions. But Daisy was barely focused on her driving. No one was currently on the road, anyway. She turned into the station parking lot, leaping out of the vehicle with the key still in the ignition.

"Can I help you?" the woman behind the counter asked when Daisy flew through the door. She wore an EMS uniform, and Daisy strained to see through the windows to the vehicle bay, searching for Luke.

"Where's Luke?"

"I'm sorry, who are you?"

"Daisy Colton. I need to find Luke Richards. I... I think he might be in trouble."

The woman furrowed her brow. "You just missed him. He was sent on a call with Squad 2 just a few minutes ago."

"Where did they go? I have to find him!" Tears ran

down Daisy's cheeks as Eric's words played over and over in her mind.

"I'm sorry, mam, I can't give out that information. If you wait here, Luke will be back—"

Daisy didn't wait. She flung the door open, running back to her car and pulling out of the parking lot.

The roads were growing slicker as Daisy drove up and down the suburban streets of Erie River. She peered down every driveway, scanned every parking lot she passed. No ambulances. She stopped at a four-way stop and took a deep breath.

"What am I doing?" she whispered, watching as her wiper blades swept back and forth across her window. The snow had mostly stopped. She flipped them to a lower setting and pulled out her phone.

Eric's messages still displayed on the screen. She was giving him power over her. He wasn't even here, and she was giving him control. Control that she had already taken back. Control that wasn't his to take anymore. But her mind was too caught up in every possible outcome, every horrible scenario an imagination that thrived on fiction books and epic movies could think of. It couldn't land on a solution.

Daisy shook her head, forcing herself to focus. She'd drive back to the station and wait for Luke. That was the simplest answer. Then, if Eric came looking for her at her mother's house, she wouldn't be there. She'd text her mother when she was safely parked at the station. Yes, that was the answer. She didn't have to do this alone.

With the snow starting to build on her windshield again, Daisy put her foot on the gas pedal. She didn't see until it was too late and plowed headlong into the side of a pickup truck. The airbags exploded in her face, and for a moment, her quick intake of breath felt stunted as the fabric collided with her face.

She barely registered that she was in an accident. Her arms felt heavy, and a sudden pain seared across her chest. She stared through her broken windshield, unable to see anything. Her purse was all over the passenger side floor, and her phone was nowhere to be found. She heard someone tap on the glass of her driver side window. An older man with a long gray beard stared down at her. It took several moments for her to find her arms, to use them. Eventually, she found the button for the window.

"Are you okay, Miss? I've called an ambulance."

An ambulance. Yes, that's what she needed. Luke and his ambulance. Because… because…

"I need to meet Luke at the ambulance," she said, her thoughts coming out in a jumble of words as the edges of her vision began to darken.

"I've got one on the way, Miss. Can you put your car in park for me?"

Daisy looked down at her gear shift, but her vision was blurring.

"No, I—I have to Luke…"

The sound of the man's voice faded as blackness

surrounded Daisy. It seemed like a lifetime later when she saw flashing lights outside the broken windshield.

"Daisy!" a familiar voice called, bringing her to focus again. "Daisy, it's Luke. You'll be okay."

Daisy turned her head, and Luke's blurry face swam before her. Yes, Luke. She needed to find Luke.

"Luke," she whispered and fell to darkness.

day 35

The gentle, steady beep of a medical machine lulled Daisy from sleep. She took a deep breath and immediately regretted it. Searing pain flashed across her sides, and she hissed through her teeth.

"Daisy? Take it easy. You're in the hospital. Daisy, can you hear me?" came a woman's condescending voice.

Daisy's eyes fluttered open. She lay in a hospital bed, hooked up to at least three different machines. The flimsy hospital gown they had dressed her in bunched in the small of her back. She shifted carefully as a blood pressure cuff inflated, squeezing her arm with more ferocity than Daisy expected. She would have ripped it off right there, but her other hand was home to an IV that dripped a clear liquid from a bag to her right.

"How are you feeling?" the nurse asked, coming to Daisy's side.

"What happened?"

The nurse casually pressed buttons on one of Daisy's machines. "You were in a car accident. You hit a truck, do you remember?"

Flashes of colliding with a pickup truck, and the aftermath of the airbag deployment went through her mind. It all happened because she was trying to find Luke.

"Luke," Daisy said. He had been there. At the very end. She remembered his voice, his face. "Where's Luke Richards?" She tried to push herself up, but the nurse set a hand on her shoulder, easing her to stay.

"We've already been in touch with your emergency contact. He's waiting out in his car per protocol. I'll have the nurse's station page him." The nurse updated her notes on the computer and left, pulling the curtain over the door.

Daisy leaned back into the thin pillow. She'd really messed up this time. Wrecking her car under a fit of sheer madness because her ex claimed he was back in town. She didn't know how she'd look Luke in the eye after this. Eric was impetuous, yes, but he wouldn't do something as rash as travel halfway across the country after her.

She heard footsteps outside the curtain. If Luke was here, it meant he still cared. She might be able to salvage this after all. Daisy pushed herself up as best she could as the curtain was pulled aside.

"What are you doing here?" she demanded, her IV

the only thing keeping her from running clear out of the room at that moment.

"Relax, it's me," Eric said, as a patronizing smile spread across his face.

"I'm well aware it's you, and I don't want you here."

Eric held up his hands, inching closer to the single chair that sat beside Daisy's bed.

"Don't say that, baby girl. You left me as your emergency contact. Surely you wanted me here. Of course, you could have just returned my messages. There was no need to be so reckless just to get me to come to you. Here, I brought you some water."

He handed her a plastic thermos from the hospital, the end of the straw bearing deep chew marks. Daisy took it and set it aside.

"Eric, I appreciate that you came all the way out here, but I meant what I said. I don't want to be in a relationship with you anymore."

"Then why would you knowingly put yourself in the hospital for me to come down here?"

"I didn't know—I didn't remember you were still listed—"

Eric pressed a finger to Daisy's lips. She pulled away but remained silent.

"Save your strength, baby girl. I've already talked to the doctor, and he's agreed to release you into my custody."

"Custody? What? I'm not a child, Eric!"

"I told you, Daisy, you aren't well. And the month

you've spent living with your mother probably hasn't helped your condition. She's such an enabler. She's dangerous to be around, Daisy."

"My condition? I don't have a condition!" The beeping of the machines around Daisy increased at a steady pace. She didn't even notice the blood pressure cuff until it released her arm and beeped a warning.

"Daisy, relax. It's okay. I forgive you. I forgive you for everything. Even Luke."

"How do you know about Luke?"

Any moment now, the nurse would come back in, and Daisy could tell her this was all a mistake.

"I know everything about your little fling, baby girl. And after the stunt you just pulled, he wants nothing to do with you."

Daisy's heart skipped a beat. "Th—that's not true."

Eric hung his head and sighed. "He was part of the team that brought you in, Daisy. He saw the whole thing and realized how mentally unstable you are. He spoke to one of the nurses, and then he just left."

Daisy's lip trembled, and she felt tears sting her eyes. "He… he was scheduled to work a double shift. H—he had to get back to work."

Eric shifted forward, taking Daisy's hand. Daisy bit her lip to stop it from shaking, but Eric's touch was all she needed for her hands to stop trembling. She hated herself for it. She hated that his touch was still comforting, that his voice was still so soothing and reassuring to her.

"That was hours ago. He hasn't come back. And Daisy, he isn't coming back. That's what guys like him do. They'll lead a vulnerable girl on, take advantage of her, and then throw her to the side when things get to be too much."

A single tear ran down Daisy's cheek. She took a deep breath, unable to stop herself. Everything hurt. Her sides, her chest. It felt like every molecule in her body had snapped like a rubber band. But her heart hurt the most. In one moment of weakness, she'd lost everything and slid right back to where she started.

"Where's my phone?" she asked, an instant of clarity coming to her, and she wiped the tears from her eyes.

"You don't need—"

"I'll call Luke. I can prove—"

"Your phone was destroyed in the crash, Daisy."

The tiny spark of hope in Daisy faded. Eric released her hand, leaning back in his chair and reaching for a copy of *Men's Fitness*. His touch lingered on her skin for longer than she cared to admit. She turned away from him, feigning sleep.

Her thoughts drifted to Luke, to everything she'd lost. Their conversations, both hysterical and deep. The way he looked at her, even through a stupid computer camera, in a way that cut to her soul. The way he spoke to her, confident and encouraging. The memory of his scent filled her, and she wished it were his touch that lingered on her.

But it was gone. All of it. She'd lost everything.

Daisy slowly turned back to Eric, watching him as he flipped through another magazine. Perhaps it was all meant to be. No matter how hard she fought it, Eric was the one.

The words of Jean de La Fontaine came to her. *A person often meets their destiny on the road they took to avoid it.* Avoiding Eric had only brought him to her. Then what did the last five weeks with Luke mean? For she had desperately tried to avoid him in the beginning too.

The curtain moved aside, pulling Daisy from her thoughts. The nurse had returned accompanied by a short, balding man.

"Hello. I'm Doctor Sherdan. Can you tell me your name?" the man asked. He handed the nurse a stack of papers, and pulled a tiny flashlight pen from his pocket, shining it at Daisy's eyes.

"Daisy Lynn Colton."

"Very good." Doctor Sherdan donned a pair of gloves and continued his tests, poking and prodding at Daisy. "How are you feeling?"

"She's a little disoriented," Eric chimed in before Daisy could answer. "I think she'll be all right."

Doctor Sherdan smiled, finishing his evaluation and disposing of the gloves before washing his hands.

"Excellent. You're pretty bruised up, but we don't believe there's any internal bleeding. Due to our current pandemic situation, we're running short on beds, so we're going to release you. Do you have someone to take care of you?"

Daisy opened her mouth, but Eric cut her off. "Yes, I'm her boyfriend. I'll be her caretaker. When will she be able to travel? We're from out of town and were just visiting family."

"How far out of town?" the nurse asked, not bothering to look up from her paperwork.

"Arizona," said Eric.

"I wouldn't suggest traveling for a day or two, but you should be fine by then," Doctor Sherdan replied, signing his name to a piece of paper the nurse handed him. "These are your discharge instructions. Information here about concussions, and the bruising you should expect from your injuries. If anything seems out of the ordinary, this is the telephone number to contact our nurse hotline." He circled a phone number at the bottom of the last page and handed the stack of papers to Eric.

The conversation ping-ponged back and forth from Eric to the doctor over Daisy's bed. She watched each in turn, one side to the other and back again, her voice falling further and further down her throat until it was practically nonexistent. She signed her name to the release forms and watched as the nurse and doctor left the room. Her last thoughts of *I don't want to leave with him* fell into silence within her own mind.

Eric helped her out of her hospital gown, his hands roaming over her bruised skin more than necessary. Daisy wanted to hate it. She wished it made her skin crawl. In a way it did, but she hadn't realized how desperate she'd been for such a touch, the kind of touch she may have had with Luke if the quarantine wasn't forcing them apart. But that future was fading more by the moment.

Eric escorted her out to his sleek, red Corvette. He helped her into the passenger seat, dictating each step before fastening the seat belt for her and abandoning the wheelchair in an empty parking spot. He climbed into the driver's seat and leaned toward Daisy.

"I've missed you, baby girl," he whispered, tucking a strand of hair behind her ear. "God, look at you. What has your mother done to you? What has that *boy* done?"

"What do you mean?" Daisy said, trying to pull away, but the seatbelt held her fast, pushing against her already sore body.

"You've gained so much weight. I can't believe your own mother didn't care enough to keep you healthy. Don't worry. We'll get you exercising again, get your roots touched up. You'll be beautiful again."

He pulled her chin toward him, pressing his lips to hers and forcing his tongue into her mouth like a savage. Pain wracked her body as he clung to her. Daisy tried to turn away, but he held her face in his hands. With what little strength she could muster, she pushed against him until he finally pulled away, and she took in a gasping breath.

"What's the matter?" he demanded, his face pulled into an accusatory grimace.

"I'm sorry," Daisy said instinctively. "The accident. I just… I hurt."

Eric released her face, pushing it away and putting the car in drive. "It's not like you don't deserve it. Karma has its way, Daisy. Next time, just return my text. It will be a lot less expensive."

He pulled out of the parking lot, stepping hard on the gas pedal and throwing Daisy back into her seat.

"Who are you staying with?" she asked quietly.

"I booked us a room at a local hotel. We can stay there a few days. We don't need to burden your mom anymore."

"I thought you said you were staying with friends."

Eric didn't answer. They turned left down a side street opposite the way back to Daisy's childhood home. She watched a streetlamp flick to life as they drove beneath. It was identical to the streetlamp outside Mrs. Frothman's house, the same one she'd stared at the night Luke played tic-tac-toe with her on the window.

The engine revved again. *A few days.* Eric said they'd stay in the hotel a few days. She had time. Beneath the red and purple bruise across her chest, hope kindled, very faintly.

Daisy flipped the light on in the dingy hotel room. It buzzed, flickering slightly before springing to life. Eric's clothes and several days' worth of fast food bags lay strewn about the room. Something that smelled suspiciously of mold struck her, and she crinkled her nose before stepping inside.

Eric smacked her rear as he entered behind her, closing the door and pushing Daisy against the wall. He kissed her again, this time more gently, his hands finding hers and holding her against the peeling wallpaper.

"You have no idea how much I've missed you," he said, his breath hot and putrid on her face.

"Eric," Daisy breathed between his tongue flicks, "Eric, I'm exhausted."

He pulled away, his eyes glassy with passion and staring through her, like he didn't even see her. "All right," he said, forcing compassion into his voice. But

Daisy knew better. She saw the slight up curl of his lip, the look of suppressed disgust.

He released her but did not back away. He pulled off his shirt, leaning in for one last nip on her neck with his teeth. Unfastening the clasp of his belt, Eric let his jeans fall to the floor where he stood. He leaned into her once more, and Daisy looked away as his fingers trailed across her body, her mind disconnecting.

"Get some sleep," he whispered in her ear. "You'll need it."

He headed toward the bathroom, leaving Daisy pressed against the wall. She crossed the room on unsteady legs, falling onto the mattress with its cigarette burns and mysterious stains. She peered in the trashcan beside the end table, noting a used condom wrapper from a brand Eric never used. He may not have stayed with friends like he claimed, but he hadn't been alone.

And that was his weakness. He couldn't handle being alone. Alone meant he wasn't needed, and Eric needed to be needed. Daisy closed her eyes, ears strained like prey against a predator. He needed to be needed, but she didn't need him anymore. She heard the squeal of the shower, the scraping of the metal shower hooks move back and forth, and she dove for Eric's jeans.

Sure enough, she pulled her new cellphone from his back pocket. Its screen was cracked, and the battery low, but it still worked. Pulling down the top menu, she read the date and time. 8:37 AM on Thursday. She'd been in the hospital a full day.

Daisy stood, searching the room until she found Eric's charger and plugged in her phone. She thanked the phone Gods for the move toward more universal charging ports as she pulled up her messages. Twelve texts from her mother, seventeen from Luke. The phone had stopped counting her missed calls after fifteen and displayed 10+ next to her voicemail box.

Mom: Are you okay? Luke told me what happened. I'm trying to get visitation rights with the hospital.

Mom: Daisy, the hospital won't let me visit. Please call me as soon as you get this.

Mom: I told Luke about Eric. Call me, please, Daisy. I left you a message.

Daisy pulled up her voicemail box, playing her mother's messages.

"Daisy, it's Mom. I tried telling the hospital about you and Eric, but they said they can't deny him seeing you because he's still listed as your emergency contact. As soon as you get this message, you need to tell them you don't want him to see you. I'm listed as secondary, but with this stupid pandemic, they're only letting one person in. Call me, please, Daisy."

"Honey, it's your mom. The hospital said you were

released. Where are you? I'll come get you. Call me."

The water in the shower still flowed. Daisy stared at the dingy carpet and sighed. She couldn't drag her mother into this. Not like this. At the edge of her mind, a plan was forming. She swiped away the voicemail application and pulled up her text messages again.

Luke: Please call me.

Luke: I was able to convince the nurse to tell me Eric is still listed as your emergency contact. I told your mom. Daisy, she told me everything he's done to you. Don't let him get to you. You're strong, Daisy.

She flipped back to her voicemails and saw a single message from Luke. Daisy pressed play and brought the phone to her ear.

"Daisy, this is Luke. I... I'm so worried about you. Please don't go back to him. You've overcome so much to start a new life, and... and even if I'm not a part of it, he doesn't deserve to be in it. You are too good for him, Daisy. You're too good for me, and I can't let you throw everything you've worked for away. Whatever you decide, I wanted you to know... you were always my first wish, Daisy. Always. Don't go back to him. I love you, Daisy."

A single tear slid down Daisy's cheek. Her learned behavior screamed his words were a lie, that it was a ploy, a trick. But she knew in her heart it was the truth. His words fanned the flame of that tiny spark that had risen inside her when they drove beneath that streetlamp. It fueled her mind to action.

Daisy wiped the tear. If she walked out that hotel door now, where would she go? She couldn't walk home from here. Eric would find her all too quickly. He'd find her walking cold and alone. He'd do something, say something. She'd almost fell for it at the hospital. She'd nearly given up hope then. Daisy couldn't break this spell alone—not entirely, at least. And she wasn't alone anymore.

The shower turned off, and Daisy's thumbs flew across the screen keyboard. She unplugged the phone, shoved it back into Eric's jeans, and sat on the end of the bed as Eric emerged moments later.

"I thought you were tired," he said, his body glistening wet.

Daisy bit her lip. "I don't want to wait," she said. "I… I want to leave now."

Eric took a step toward her, the towel wrapped around his waist threatening to fall. "But the doctor said—"

"I feel fine, I promise. I—I want to pretend this never happened. I want to start over." She couldn't look at him as she spoke. She'd never been an adept liar.

Eric smirked, lifting Daisy's chin up to look at him. She took a breath, forcing herself to believe she was looking into Luke's eyes, forcing herself to recall the scent of bergamot and oakmoss, forcing away the fear that rose in her chest.

"That's the smartest thing you've said all day." He leaned down to her, pushing her back on the bed and kissed her again. She gave in, and though her body lay on a gritty bedspread in a dank hotel room, her mind wandered to places where Luke stood outside her window, drawing hearts instead of circles, and where a strand of dark brown hair fell across hazel eyes.

Eric pulled away. "You've never kissed me like that before," he said.

Daisy opened her eyes, hiding her disappointment at seeing Eric's face above hers. "Like I said, I want to start over."

He leaned down again, but Daisy pushed him off. "Come on, get dressed," she said, wielding the authority she'd found in Eric's absence. "My mom and Luke are still at work. We'll be long gone before they even realize it."

"Whatever you say, baby girl." He climbed off her, letting the towel fall to the floor.

Daisy let her eyes linger over his body and forced a smile, hoping the gesture was convincing enough to stroke his ego and keep him moving. He winked and began dressing.

The snow had ceased falling, leaving behind a blanket of dampness across the world and tiny white pillows in the shade of the trees and houses. Eric drove his Corvette through the streets of uptown Erie River, taking every opportunity to rev his engine, and smiling smugly each time. He reached for Daisy's hand, bringing it to rest just inside his thigh.

"I'm glad you came to your senses, Daisy," Eric said, rubbing his thumb against the back of her hand. "Maybe this accident was a blessing. Whatever was wrong with you, that knock on your head straightened you out."

"Mhm..." Daisy nodded, barely listening as he droned on.

"… but my mother, she raised me right. She taught me to respect women, to take care of them because they aren't smart enough to take care of themselves. Women need someone to guide them. And it's not your fault, you know. You didn't pick your genes."

"You're right. I didn't pick my genes."

Genes that gave her her mother's ash-blonde hair, and her father's kindness. Genes that allowed her to eat cheese without becoming ill, and genes that let her hide her thoughts behind a mask. Eric droned on, and Daisy couldn't help but smile. He was right—she didn't pick her genes. Nor could he change them.

"Yeah, exactly. And I get why you ran away. You wanted one last adventure. One last time living your childhood fantasies. I should have been more supportive. I should have come with you."

"Well, you're here now." Daisy smiled, gently sliding her hand closer to Eric's knee.

They pulled onto High Street, Daisy's head throbbing as the g-force pushed her body back into her seat. With each house they passed, each green lawn that brought her closer to her home, her heart beat faster. She'd done this once before, she could do it again.

Eric pulled into the empty driveway, bringing the car to a stop with a jolt that made Daisy's sides burn with pain. She winced, but didn't immediately reach for her seatbelt.

You can do this. But what if she didn't want to? Was it easier to let Eric tell her what to do? Was it more convenient not having to make decisions on her own? She glanced in the side mirror at Luke's empty driveway and saw Apollo's head peeking between the curtains of the front window.

"Ready?" Eric asked.

Daisy pulled her hand from his knee. "Yeah. I'll be right back."

"I can help—"

"It's okay," Daisy said, opening the car door. "I didn't bring very much. Maybe I always knew I'd be coming back."

Eric shrugged as Daisy closed the door. She walked up the front path lined with its overflowing garden of flowers. Little patches of snow still clung to the base of the front steps. She reached for the door handle and turned.

"Eric?"

He rolled down his window, his brows furrowed.

"Can… can we get pizza later."

He hesitated. "I… guess. What kind of question is that?"

"I'm just hungry."

Shrugging, Eric pressed the button to roll up his window.

"Eric!" Daisy called again.

Eric rolled his eyes, bringing the window back down. "What?"

"With pineapple?"

"What? Daisy, are you sure you're up to traveling?"

"On the pizza. Can I get pineapple on the pizza?"

"Yeah, sure. As much as you want. You like pineapple on your pizza."

Daisy nodded. She swallowed, flashing Eric a smile

before stepping inside.

The house was eerily quiet, save for the little black kitten that meowed in protest at her feet. She took Pepper into her arms, carrying the cat through the home as she walked from room to room.

Everything she'd experienced in her life, every condescending remark, every opportunity to pull herself back up, had all been for this. The daisy's petals would unfold, pure white amidst an unpredictable climate, year after year.

She turned into her childhood bedroom and stared at the unfinished mural by her bed. The collage of magazine clippings of Orlando Bloom lay neatly folded into a box beneath her bed, a treasure to one day find and remember.

Pepper jumped from her arms, peering down the hall with a low growl.

"Geez, Daisy!" Eric said, and Daisy jumped. "When did you get a cat?"

Pepper hissed and disappeared under the dresser. His grumbling growl reverberated through the room, green eyes glowing from the darkness.

"Oh, he... he's Mom's cat," Daisy said, dragging her suitcase from the closet.

"Good, because you know it's not coming with us."

Daisy didn't answer.

"Did you paint that?" Eric continued, staring up at the mural and running his hand along the top of his head.

"Yeah. Not bad, huh?"

Eric scoffed. "For an amateur, I guess." He shrugged, turning to Daisy and flashing a smile. "Hey, don't worry! I'll get your job back at the restaurant. You'll be back to what you're good at in no time." He kissed her, and Pepper's growling deepened.

"I'll be out in five minutes," she said, pushing against his chest. "I... I want to say goodbye."

"I'm setting a timer on my phone. Five minutes."

Daisy heard his footsteps fade away down the hall and heard the front door slam close. Five minutes might not be enough time. She bolted down the hall and through the kitchen. She threw open the back door, dashing across the yard. She picked her way carefully through the tulips and crocus, headed for Mrs. Frothman's backyard.

"Daisy!" Mrs. Colton stood from a plastic lawn chair on their neighbor's patio and ran to her daughter. She wrapped her arms around Daisy, who pulled away at the last moment when her mother squeezed her still tender bruises. "I thought I lost you again."

Daisy pushed away the lump in her throat. "No, Mama. I'm not going anywhere. Do you have the number pulled up just in case?"

Mrs. Colton nodded, and her eyes grew suddenly wide as she stared over Daisy's shoulder.

"What are you doing?" came Eric's voice. His calm facade replaced with anger, ready to boil over.

Daisy's jaw clenched as she turned to face him, her

mother's hand holding tight to her own.

"I'm leaving, Eric," she said, her voice trembling as Mrs. Colton's hand gave a reassuring squeeze.

"No, that's what you're supposed to be doing. You lied to me, Daisy. You said your mom was at work. What's going on?"

"I'm leaving *you*, Eric. It's over."

Eric's mouth fell open. He blinked slowly, processing the situation. He shifted his weight, relaxing his shoulders, and holding out his hands to her.

"Baby girl, don't listen—"

"Do *not* call me that! I am no one's baby. Especially yours." Daisy cleared her throat, forcing down the pitch in her voice. "Give me my phone, and leave."

"Daisy," Eric said, taking a step toward her, his hands still outstretched in a placating gesture. "Come on. You're just confused. Come here. I'll take care of you. I can fix you."

"She doesn't need fixing!" Mrs. Colton snapped.

Daisy squeezed her mother's hand, silencing her. "I'm not confused, Eric. And you're the one who's lied. Now, give me my phone in your back pocket and leave."

Eric took another step forward and opened his mouth to speak.

"You heard the lady." Luke stepped into view from the side yard. He stood tall, his Captain America shirt stretched across his chest. His hazel eyes locked with Daisy, and he gave a single nod of acknowledgment to her, his strength replenishing her strength.

"Oh, I see what's going on," Eric said, his voice breaking as he spoke. "You bring your new boy toy here to do your work for you. I thought we were moving past this, Daisy. I thought you'd come to your senses. Now I see you need other people to fight your battles for you. I told you, you were weak."

"She doesn't need anyone to fight for her, and if you were half as smart as she is, you'd not only see that, but you'd still be back in Arizona," Luke said, taking a step closer to Eric.

"Jealous type are we? Daisy, get over here now. We're leaving."

"No, Eric." She turned to Luke again and nodded. Luke nodded back, retreating a few steps as Daisy released her mother's hand. "I asked Luke and Mom to be here not because I needed someone to fight my battles for me, but because I wanted witnesses."

"Witnesses? Daisy, I've never laid a finger on you! How could you—"

Daisy raised her hand, the gesture catching Eric off guard and silencing him mid-word. "I wanted witnesses to see what you've done to me, and how I broke free. I didn't need them here to tell you I'm done, to tell you I never want to see you again. I *wanted* them here because I don't have to do this alone anymore. You isolated me. You took me away from everyone I ever loved, and you kept me away. You kept me in a little cage to do and say and be whatever you wanted.

No more, Eric. I am *done*. Now, hand me my phone before my witnesses give testimony to the authorities my mother has on speed dial."

Mrs. Colton flashed a sneering smirk, waving her phone at Eric from where she stood behind Daisy.

"This is just a mistake. You're confused, Daisy." Eric's voice caught in his throat. He looked from one face to the next, panic setting into the lines around his eyes and mouth.

"You were the mistake, Eric."

"No!" Eric charged forward, trampling through the flowerbed toward Daisy. "I'm not driving all the way out here for nothing!" He grabbed Daisy's arm, pushing Mrs. Colton to the side.

"Hey!" Luke shouted, but it wasn't at Eric.

A mass of fur collided with Daisy's legs, knocking Eric back. Apollo stood between them, teeth bared and growling like Daisy had never heard him before.

"Call it off!" Eric shrieked.

"I don't think so," Luke said, crossing his arms. "This is your last warning."

"What the—" Eric stumbled sideways, releasing Daisy's arm and tripping over Pepper who had snuck out the back door. The smell of concentrated cat urine filled the air, and even Apollo sneezed between growls.

"Fine! But when you find out what's out here, what the world is really like, you'll come crawling back to me. You'll be begging me to take you back!" He threw Daisy's phone at Luke and limped toward his red

Corvette, shaking his soaked pant leg.

They all watched as the car whipped out of the drive, speeding down the street with its engine revving in rage. Daisy barely noticed when Apollo sat at Luke's feet, happily wagging his tail and licking at the strings of slobber hanging from his mouth. She barely noticed when Mrs. Colton petted Pepper, giving an off-hand remark about how she never thought delaying his neuter would have turned out to be a good thing. She listened until the sound of the Corvette's engine faded into silence.

Daisy turned to Luke, who still stood on the other side of the flowerbed, scratching Apollo's ear. A shadow of stubble was visible along his jawline, and that single strand of hair still fell across his eyes. He smiled at her, and she didn't need to hear him say the words.

Forget social distancing.

It felt like her feet barely touched the ground as she covered the distance between them. Luke didn't wait. He met her halfway, taking her into his arms and holding her.

Daisy buried her face in his shoulder. "Thank you," she whispered.

Luke continued to hold her, speaking softly, his warm breath tickling her neck. "For what?"

"For believing in me. For helping me believe in myself."

Luke pulled back, looking into her eyes. He brushed her cheek with his fingertips. "Parting is such sweet sorrow, Juliet. I couldn't bear the morrow without you." His eyes glanced briefly at her lips, and Daisy leaned into him. Her mouth brushed against his, slow and searching. He let her take the lead as he cupped her cheek in his hand.

Daisy pulled away, taking a breath.

"Did I hurt you?" Luke asked, loosening his hold on her.

Daisy smiled, holding tighter to him in return. "No, it wasn't that."

"What?"

Daisy bit her lip, her cheeks flushing with more than just passion now. "Remember the line at the end of *The Princess Bride?*"

"Since the invention of the kiss—"

Daisy lifted a finger to Luke's lips.

"I was just thinking. Wesley's got nothing on Luke Richards."

He ran his fingers through her hair, and she tilted her chin up to meet his lips again. He handled her with such gentleness and such passion, Daisy thought she might collapse if she wasn't holding onto him. This is what she'd waited for, what she thought only existed in fairy tales.

Apollo whined at their feet. Luke and Daisy turned to see him staring at Mrs. Colton's retreating back as she carried Pepper quietly toward the back door. They smiled at each other, and Luke took Daisy's hand. As they headed back to the house, Daisy caught movement over her shoulder. She turned and saw Mrs. Frothman's curtain shift. Except this time, the old woman stood behind it and gave the girl a wink.

day 491

Fifteen Months Later

Daisy dipped her brush in the paint again, carefully adding shading to the Batman logo she'd painted on the study room wall. It faced the Doors of Durin on the opposite wall she'd painted last week. She scratched at her arm, the site where she'd received her final vaccine. It stung beneath her bandage as she raised her arm to continue her project.

Apollo lifted his head from where he slept in the doorway, giving a low grumble before taking off into the living room. Pepper followed close behind, and Daisy heard the front door open moments later.

"How's my boys!" Luke said from the other room.

Daisy heard Apollo dancing and yipping in excited circles around him. She rinsed her brush, wiping her hands and carefully stepping over her palette of paints.

"Where for art thou, Juliet!" Luke called.

Daisy poked her head out of the room. "I have a surprise for you," she said, motioning with a single finger for Luke to come.

Luke grabbed her hand, pulling Daisy into him and kissing her. "You mean you're not my surprise?"

Daisy giggled. "It shouldn't be a surprise to find me at home. Or did you forget I live here now?"

"This is true, but I'll never take it for granted." He kissed her again and released her.

Daisy covered Luke's eyes with her hands and led him through to the study room, Apollo and Pepper trailing close behind. She turned him to face the wall she'd been painting and lifted her hands.

Luke's mouth fell open. "You finished it?"

"Yep! Well, almost."

"Daisy! But I thought you had your chemistry and baking finals today."

Daisy leaned against the doorframe, arms crossed, and a smirk on her face. "I did. And I'm pretty sure I aced them. I was the third one finished in the entire class, so I had some extra time today."

Luke lifted her into his arms, and Daisy wrapped her legs around his waist, laughing.

"I love it when you giggle like that. And I love the mural. Thank you." He kissed her again, this one slow and passionate. She kissed him back, allowing herself to sink into the fiery desire she'd never felt until she met him.

"You're incredible," Luke murmured against her lips. "I love you."

"I know," Daisy breathed.

Other books from White Whisker Publications

THE SILVER FOX MYSTERIES
(published under C.P. Morgan)

Dorothy Claes and the Prison of Thenemi
Dorothy Claes and the Prowl of the Yule Cat
Dorothy Claes and the Blood of the Tsar

THE KINGDOMS OF CHARTILE
(published under Cassandra Morgan)

Prophecy
Magic